"WE ARE UNDER ATTACK, CAPTAIN. . . ."

"Weapons control," said a crisp, business-like voice. "Missiles have been fired. Six incoming. Vectors—"

"Shields up," Josh ordered.

A tingling sensation at the back of his neck told him that the computer had responded to his order.

"Weapons," Josh barked, "have you determined the origin of the missiles?"

"That is affirmative," Weapons said. "Viewscreen three, sir."

Josh lifted his head. On the screen, made small by distance, was a compact vehicle with lines that were totally unfamiliar.

"Missiles incoming," Weapons said. "Range five miles."

"All right, Weapons, let's see if we can cool this fellow's jets a bit. . . ."

DEEP FREEZE

ZACH HUGHES

DAW BOOKS, INC.

DONALD A. WOLLHEIM, FOUNDER

375 Hudson Street, New York, NY 10014

ELIZABETH R. WOLLHEIM
SHEILA E. GILBERT
PUBLISHERS

First Printing, November 1992

1 2 3 4 5 6 7 8 9

DAW TRADEMARK REGISTERED
U.S. PAT OFF AND FOREIGN COUNTRIES
—MARCA REGISTRADA,
HECHO EN U.S.A.

PRINTED IN THE U.S.A.

CHAPTER ONE

Dan Webster came into the control room wearing gym shorts. He had a towel draped around his neck. Sweat gleamed on his chest and shoulders.

"Nice of you to decide to join me," his wife said. "Not that it's anything of priority. Certainly not as important as your daily exercise."

Dan grinned. "I did detect a certain amount of urgency in your voice, Mama."

"Don't call me Mama," she said. "I am not your mother."

"Thank God," he said. He came to stand behind her. "With this machine it is impossible to get lost."

Fran Webster lifted her eyebrows and said, "Tell that to the machine."

"Let me take a look. Let's see what you've done wrong," Dan said, taking Fran's place in the command chair and swiveling it toward the console of the Century Series computer.

Fran said, "Hummmph."

Dan reached out to pat her on her soft rump. Touching her renewed his awareness that at an age which represented almost three quarters of her life expectancy—and his—she was still shapely and firm, but there would be time for that. There was always plenty of time when two people alone on a small ship set out to cover considerable distances across the emptiness of space. At the moment it was of interest to find out why the computer was confused.

He was a tall man, Dan Webster, a smiling man. Although in a certain light his pale scalp gleamed on the back of his head he still had most of his hair. The decades had been kind to him. Fran, almost as tall as he, had a mature figure. She was an attractive woman. Her brown hair was just beginning to lighten with gray. She pinched him playfully as she moved aside to let him take the command chair.

"Now the thing to remember," Dan said, "is not to push any buttons until you know exactly what buttons to push. As they taught us, you've got to remember the proper buttonology." So saying, he pushed a button that caused an explosion of telltale trouble lights on the display.

"I do like to learn from an expert," Fran said smugly.

Dan grinned widely. "Just giving you a demonstration of what not to do."

He corrected his error and punched in the Navpro. As the old Century Series computer began to muck around in its Verbolt Cloud memory chambers it made a sound so much like a labored grunt that Dan pulled back, startled. Star maps began to flash on and off the display with dizzying speed.

"Come on now," Dan said, pressing buttons soothingly. The computer's frantic searchings slowed, but the star fields on the display bore no resemblance to the dots and blazes of light visible on the optic viewscreen over Dan's head.

"I told you," Fran said. "I said, Papa, if we're going to go jumping off into unexplored space on a little ship not much bigger than my dressing room at home, I think we'd better have a new computer."

"Yes, Mama, that's what you said," Dan sighed, as he spoke comforting things to the computer through his fingertips.

"Staying close to home wasn't adventurous enough for Mr. Daniel Webster. No, sir. Taking a nice vacation on Terra II or one of the nice new wilderness worlds wasn't for him. He had to go where no one else had gone. He had to spend all sorts of money on—what?" She paused. Actually, there was no venom in her comments. They had been together for seventy years. She had borne him two sons and three daughters, all of them doing quite well, thank you, and she'd been just as eager as he to have one last little adventure before settling down into that final quarter of man's allocated six-score years.

"I spent a considerable sum of money on the *Rimfire* charts," Dan said patiently. "But not, as a certain person has hinted, enough to cause us to spend our last years in privation."

Fran looked upward. "He spent it on charts that show nothing but exit and entry points into completely unexplored segments of the galaxy," Fran said to the ship, to the humming little mechanisms, to the purring power of the blink generator, and to the expanse of unknown stars that glittered like hard diamonds on the black background of nothingness.

"Ah," Dan said, caressing a button that changed the search mode of the computer. "Look here, Mama. Somehow or other you hit this white button. See?"

"I see."

"And when you hit it you started the computer working on charts for the other side of the galaxy."

"Mummmmph," Fran said.

"The computers couldn't locate us because it was looking for us on the wrong charts."

The *Rimfire* charts were so voluminous that they had been clouded in sectors. *Rimfire,* in her time the most advanced ship in the fleet of the Department of Exploration and Alien Search, had circumnavigated the galaxy, making short excursions into promising looking areas along the periphery. She had marked her trail carefully with blink beacons. With her charts it was possible for a ship, even a small, antiquated Mule like Dan and Fran's *Old Folks,* to blink all the way around the disc of the Milky Way in a few hundred settings of the generator.

At first it had been a bit spooky making the long, long jumps outside the disc of the galaxy. Even a gentleman amateur space traveler like Dan Webster knew the fundamental rules governing the use of a blink generator. Rule number one: Never blink into the unknown. Odd things happen when a ship traveling in that never-never land that is outside of but concurrent with space and time comes into contact with an object of mass. Certain alterations in molecular bondings merge the two masses.

Everyone who had ever read anything about space travel had seen the pictures of the two known incidents of a blinking ship fusing with another body. In sculptured detail the sleek prow of a small X&A cruiser protruded from the iron-black, metallic mass of an asteroid. In even more dramatic pictures the colonizer ship *Vulpecula Columbus* was shown blended with a smaller merchantman. Bonding with a chunk of rock, an iron asteroid, or any sizable body contacted in nonspace was a terminal process for human life.

Unless X&A had laid down blink beacons one never blinked beyond the range of the ship's eyes. So, at first, making those megaleaps out there in the blackness of intergalactic space had been spooky, with *Old Folks* reluctant to leave the frail security of a blink beacon from which the view of the galaxy was more than spectacular. Off on the port quarter could be seen the galaxy's hot heart bulging in a globular mass from the slightly tilted plane of the disc. Later, as Dan grew more accustomed to blinks measured in parsecs, he was tempted to follow *Rimfire*'s trail all the way around the galaxy.

"Be something, Mama, to say we've made it all the way. Not many can say that."

"I can think of other things I'd rather say," Fran said.

Old Folks was out there in the big dark because Dan Webster wasn't ready to don house slippers and become an old man. He had worked sixty-five years with United Tigian Shipping, a firm that sent ships blinking out to every inhabited world in the United Planets sector. He had started with the company as a trainee bookkeeper and had retired a vice president with a desire to do something other than take up a hobby and wait for his personal support system to begin to malfunction. To his surprise and pleasure, it was Fran who suggested, "Papa, why don't we do some traveling?"

The ship had made a ninety-degree arc around the periphery from its point of exit opposite Tigian II. Back there on the "world" the Webster home was sealed against intruders, climate conditioned against damp or dry or mildew or gnawing insects. It could be opened only by a voice command from Dan or, in the event of necessity, an override of the security system directed by the eldest Webster son.

They had spent two months on Xanthos, the U.P. administration planet, fighting government red tape to get the final permits on the reconditioned space tug, and then they had done some simple blinking, following well established routes toward the periphery. And now *Old Folks* was a long way from home and had made a shallow penetration into an area of thinly placed stars. She rested within visual range of the blink beacon that marked *Rimfire*'s deepest excursion into the disc at that point.

"Well, Mama," Dan said, after the computer had located them precisely, showing *Old Folks* as a blinking dot amid a field of scattered stars, "where do we go from here?"

Fran shrugged.

"You've always been the lucky one," Dan said. "Pick us a winner."

"There," Fran whispered, as if in doubt. She pointed out a grouping of stars a few parsecs toward galactic center.

"There it shall be," Dan said.

They didn't even have names, that grouping of seven stars toward which *Old Folks* made her slow way. Masses of stars and interstellar matter blocked them from the telescopes on the U.P. worlds. They showed on the new *Rimfire* charts, but there had been no attempt by Captain Julie Roberts or her scientific team to name the millions of stars recorded by the ship's instruments.

Dan didn't know the procedures for naming new stars, and he didn't give it too much thought beyond an idle speculation that it would be nice to name a real pretty one for Fran. He was too busy using the ship's sensors and detectors to make sure that the next short blink didn't put *Old Folks* into the nuclear furnace of a sun or merge her with a hard, cold asteroid.

The real work began when the ship left *Rimfire*'s well marked trail. The blink generator aboard *Old Folks* had traveled not a few parsecs, for sure, but it was solid and dependable and it was powerful, for the ship was a space tug, built to take vessels a thousand times her mass into her electronic embrace and blink them safely to the nearest shipyard. The generator was capable of multiple short blinks without recharging, but even so, she spent long hours drifting in the big empty while the generator reached out to the odd mixture of magnetic and radioactive energy emanating from the nearest star.

Since there was no real hurry, they didn't work in shifts. When it was bedtime in the Western Standard Zone on Tigian II, they put the ship's systems on auto and went to sleep. Dan Webster had always looked on bedtime as one of the highlights of his day, for it meant cuddling up to the sleek softness of the woman who had carried his children. Bedtime, depending on Fran's hormonal state, could be a sweet, touching, drowsy sinking into sleep or a mutually satisfying if ritualized romp which ended with Fran making little moaning sounds and Dan laughing like a fool. He always laughed because it was so very good. After so many years they read each other's little signals, responded eagerly, and proved with surprising regularity that youth had no monopoly on the pleasures of the flesh.

Old Folks was provisioned for a voyage of three years, with emergency space rations for another half year. The Century 4000 held the largest collection of books and films available from the Library of the Confederation on Xanthos. Dan was in no hurry at all. He let the ship's detection systems minutely search the space around a near star and logged the results carefully into the computer's avid maw. It made him feel good. He hadn't discovered anything, not yet, but he was the first man to record that a particular star at a particular coordinate in space had no spawn, that nothing orbited the nuclear furnace but a band of diffuse gases and some almost undetectable floes of space dust.

Fran had attended a good school on Tigian II. Her degree was in the field of literature. She had always felt a bit guilty as she reared her family and made a home for them for not having continued her school days delving into the "better" books produced by the writers of the hundreds of worlds that made up the United Planets Confederation. She had promised herself that she'd use the time in space to catch up on her reading, but so far, she had not made it through one book. The stilted language didn't ring well in her ears. The concerns of the writers of a thousand years in the past seemed, in the light of real life, to be inconsequential. Now, as *Old Folks* blinked in short jumps toward a G-class star a few light-years away from the first sun examined by the ship's sensors, she decided that she would do a paper for publication by her discussion group on the works and career of a particular holofilm director. This gave her an excuse to watch her very favorite films over and over, eased the irritation of having to make selections from the almost too complete collection in the computer chambers, and drove Dan to catch up on his exercise in the ship's gym.

When Dan called his wife away from her fourth viewing of her favorite of all favorite films she saw immediately that he was excited.

"Look, Frannie," he said, pointing to the screen.

"Oh, my," Fran said.

By optical tricks the ship's eyes showed a little yellow star and its family of no less than six planets. By compressing the distances between the orbiting bodies the optics made the grouping look like a model solar system in a classroom.

"Oh, my, Daniel," Fran said.

"I have to confess, Frannie, that I didn't have too much confidence that we'd actually find something," Dan said.

She bent quickly and kissed him. "Dan Webster, you've always accomplished everything you set out to do."

"Then I guess I set my aim too low, huh, Mama?"

"You hush. And don't call me Mama."

"Well, there they are. Like a hen and her chicks." He chuckled. "Which one shall we name Frannie's World?"

"That would be a silly name for a planet."

"Not in my opinion," he said. He turned to the console. "Let's take a closer look."

Two of the outer planets were dark and ice-shrouded, far from the life-giving warmth of the sun, circling the distant source like unwanted orphans. The next two, as they were enlarged on the viewer, proved to be gas giants. The first planet was too near the solar furnace and was nothing more than scorched rock. Dan had purposely saved the second planet for last viewing, because some quick measurements by the sensors had shown the world to lie in what the computer calculated to be the little yellow sun's life zone.

Dan held his breath. He pushed buttons. The Century 4000 grunted and moaned a bit and then the image of a world began to form on the screen. Dan wanted to see the blue of a water world so badly that for a few moments the slowly turning world took on a pale hue of that most wonderful of colors. He ordered the computer to check focus. He shielded his eyes as brilliant reflected sunlight gleamed on the screen before the optics could make a corrective adjustment.

Fran's World, the second planet of a G-class star, was a spheroid of glimmering ice. There was water on the world, but it was locked into a mass of snow and ice that covered the surface almost evenly. Dan was so disappointed that he turned off the viewer and punched up a drink.

Fran came to stand beside him, pressing her soft flank against him. "There are the mining rights," she said.

"Yes, we can file for discoverer's royalty on any useful minerals," Dan said.

"Papa, how many stars have we examined?"

"Two."

"Don't you remember what we read? People who make a profession of exploration can go for decades without finding a star that has planets."

"Thank you," Dan said, patting her. "You always know what I'm thinking, don't you?"

She laughed. "Well, if I don't know you by now—"

"Some useful heavy metals may have boiled to the surface on the first planet," Dan said.

"We haven't checked for moons around the gas giants, either."

"You're right. Let's have a look."

It took some sublight maneuvering to examine the several moons of the large planets. A couple of them looked promising. Dan named five of them after his children, and applied the names of some of the grandchildren to the others. Deciding which moon to name after which child was a fun thing. The investigations of the moons filled a couple of months. They went about it in a leisurely fashion, taking time to get a full night's sleep, time to watch a film together, time to snuggle close in their large bed and do interesting things.

Old Folks edged cautiously into the solar storm of particles to come near enough to the one planet to record some encouraging readings of heavy metals, then got the hell out of there quickly, for the ship's radiation detectors were getting a bit worried. Dan parked the ship in an orbit around the second planet while he readied his claims for filing. *Old Folks* would have to blink back within range of the first *Rimfire* beacon before the announcement of discovery and the proper forms could be blinked back down the long line of beacons to X&A Headquarters on Xanthos. The temporary beacons left behind by *Old Folks* to guide them back to the beaten path could not handle blink messages.

With everything in readiness, Dan took one last look at the second planet. He set the computer to work confirming her distance from her sun and the strength of the star's radiations. He was not an astrophysicist, but he had a gut feeling that something was wrong with the figures. The second planet was roughly the same size as Tigian II. She was at an optimum distance from her sun. There were no dark and brooding clouds to shield her from the sun's life-giving emanations. When the computer confirmed once more that by all rights the water that was locked up in the vast fields of ice should have been liquid, Dan took *Old Folks* down toward the glittering surface for a closer look.

Fran watched nervously as the squarish Mule lowered until she was moving over the surface at a rate of speed that made her motion quite apparent. In open space one never realized that the ship was moving so fast.

"What are you doing, Papa?" she asked nervously.

"Just having a look."

He had all of the ship's sensors at work. A long, rounded ridge of ice was a range of impressive mountains. Lower, flatter areas made Dan wonder if once there had been oceans on Fran's World. He let the little ship zip around the planet in an orbit that eventually covered all of the surface. There were no spectacular readings, nothing to cause the systems to shout "Eureka!" with buzzers and flashing lights, but when Dan studied the readings after moving the ship into a higher, stable orbit he whistled.

"Have a look at this, Mama," he said.

"I see it," Fran said. "But what is it?" She was unable to make anything of the charted readings.

"Metals," Dan said. "Concentrations of them here and here." He pointed to two spots on the featureless globe. "Other places, too. This might be quite something, Mama. How'd you like to be very, very rich?"

"I would rather have been very, very rich when we were young," she said with a smile.

"But you wouldn't object to being rich now, I take it."

"Not too much."

Dan began to give the computer orders.

"You're not going down?" Fran asked in alarm.

"It's all right."

"There's nothing there but ice."

"Mama, it's colder in space than it will be on the surface. There's some solar heating."

"Why must we go down?"

"Because we want to be rich," he said. "Because I need better readings of those metal sources. I can get them by driving a heat probe through the ice."

Fran was still doubtful. She watched nervously as *Old Folks* lowered into a hint of atmosphere and then landed on the gleaming, icy surface.

It was not necessary for Dan to leave the ship. *Old Folks* was equipped with some basic exploratory tools, one of which was a probe that punched its way easily through two hundred feet of ice in less than an hour.

"Wow," Dan said, as the instruments recorded the nearness of masses of metal, ore so pure that he couldn't believe it. There was so much of it and so many metals were mixed together that all he got on the locater was a big mass of light.

He directed the probe to bend and melt its way toward the nearest metallic mass.

"I really don't understand this," he said.

The probe was within feet of something that showed on the instruments as a great heap of metals.

"Dan, I'm cold," Fran said, clasping her arms.

"Your imagination, Mama," Dan said. "The ice is outside."

Fran shivered. The probe neared the source of the fantastically high metallic readings. Dan, himself, felt a chill, looked up to see that Fran was shivering.

"Papa, let's go."

"Yes."

He reached. His hand froze. He felt a deadness creeping up his arm. He cried out. His breath made a cloud of vapor that froze instantly. Fran toppled, crashing stiffly to the deck. Dan reached for the panic button. His finger made contact, but he was so numb that he wasn't sure he actually pushed the button that would send a call for help beaming outward from *Old Folks*. He managed to fall beside the woman he had loved since he was sixteen, taking her into his arms with the last of his strength as the terrible cold penetrated into his stomach. He could not feel her. He wanted to weep.

The water in the tanks froze and burst the containment bulkheads. Rime formed on the outer hull. Motion in the computer's Verbolt Cloud chambers began to slow. Metals were weakened as temperatures dropped toward and past the cold of empty space. The hull crumbled and the air gushed out to freeze into drifting clouds that soon sank to the permanent snow cover and became a part of it. Over a period of months *Old Folks* collected crystals of ice from the thin atmosphere and whitened to become nothing more than a lump on the smoothness of the plain of ice. On a line toward the periphery the temporary beacons left behind by Dan Webster to guide him back to *Rim-fire*'s routes began to lose power and fail one by one. No trace of *Old Folks* remained. The only hint as to her final resting place was a nodule of ice protruding from the smoothness of the snows.

CHAPTER TWO

David Webster tried to get back to Tigian II once every three years. He had missed that goal by ten months when he blinked a sleek, new, Zede-built executive liner into a holding position over the T-Town Interplanetary Spaceport and contacted T-Town Control to report arrival and ask for landing instructions. He had named the multimillion credit ship the *Fran Webster,* for his mother, and he was looking forward to showing it to her.

Since the *Fran Webster* shouted money to anyone who knew ships, she attracted her share of attention. The young man who met David on the pad at the foot of the boarding ladder was full of questions, questions that David answered patiently as he was driven toward the terminal, for he could remember when he had worked at the T-Town port and when his goal had been to board a ship, any ship that was going to blink anywhere away from Tigian II.

"Yep," David said, "The Zedes build a good ship." He had sold his last cargo to a jewel broker in the Zede League and, to his own surprise, he had come away with the Zede-built Starliner. He had had no intention of buying a new ship. His

Little David, a civilian conversion of an X&A scout, had been only five years old and he was very fond of it. The difference between fondness and love became apparent when he took one look at the Zede Starliner.

He didn't often do business with the Zede worlds. In spite of their having been absorbed into the United Planets Confederation well over a thousand years past, the worlds and the people of the Zede systems were vaguely, inexplicably alien. It was difficult to get anyone to talk about it openly, but, even after a thousand years, there was still deep-seated resentment over the loss of a war that the Zedes had started and which the U.P. ended with a devastating salvo of planet busters. But, yes, indeed, they built a good ship, especially when money was no object and the buyer wanted every luxury that could be packed into a liner.

"Anything we can do, Captain Webster, in the way of servicing your ship?" the young driver asked.

"Thank you, no," David said.

"If there's anything, anything at all, just let me know. Ask for Pete."

"I'll do it, Pete," David said.

The young driver fell silent when David pulled out his communicator and punched in a call. The call went through four exchanges before David was connected with the proper department at X&A Tigian.

"My name is David Webster, pilot's license number TG2-7L90-300. I want to record ownership of a Zede Starliner, serial number 789—"

"Hold on, Captain Webster."

He held. The boy, Pete, pulled the groundcar to a stop at a private entrance to the T-Town Space Terminal.

"Hope you're not in a hurry," David said as he waited.

"Not at all, sir."

"Captain David Webster, TG2-7L90-300?"

"Correct."

"There is an urgent for you."

David felt a little tinge of apprehension. "Yes?"

"It's six months old, Captain Webster." The speaker was a female of pleasant voice and some sensitivity. "Perhaps you have already received it."

"No, I haven't," David said.

"The message, which went out on all routes, is from a Miss Ruth Webster," the voice said. "She requests that you return to Tigian II as quickly as possible."

"And that's it?"

"That's it."

"Thank you. I imagine that the urgent was addressed to the *Little David*."

"Yes, sir."

So that was why he hadn't received it. His old ship had been left on Zede IV and even as he had lifted off in the new Starliner the *Little David* was undergoing renovation and renaming. "May we finish registration of my new ship?" he asked politely.

"Yes, sir."

He made one more call, to his sister, Ruth.

"I'm glad you're home, David," Ruth said in

her deep, pleasant voice. "How soon can you get here?"

"Half an hour. Shall I meet you at the house?" He spoke of his parents' house, his childhood home, Ruth's childhood home.

"No. Please come to my place."

He fought back the urge to ask her what was wrong. He didn't want to hear it by communicator.

Tigian City, T-Town, was humming with activity. Ground and aircars purred, zipped, soared, sank, rose, stopped, started, darted in and out of exits. There was a smell in the air, hints of things industrial, of crowded habitation, a smell that made David pleasantly nostalgic. He was carrying only his overnight case containing toothbrush, razor, and other items of personal hygiene. He ordered up an aircar and placed a call from the passenger's seat to an old-line men's store which had records of his body measurements and his tastes. He believed in traveling light. A couple of changes of clothing with the appropriate auxiliary items, underwear, socks, would be delivered to his sister's house not long after his own arrival.

He cringed down in the seat as the aircar avoided total catastrophe with a deft maneuver. The driver had the controls on manual.

"You don't use auto?" he asked, getting just a little concerned.

"Not when it's quiet like this," the driver said, soaring to the left to avoid flying into the flux outlets of a public transporter.

David's last trip had covered parsecs running into four figures. *Little David* had landed on half a hundred outpost worlds, had flown approaches through belts of whizzing asteroids. There wasn't a flying problem in space that David Webster couldn't have handled, but T-Town aircar traffic caused him to close his eyes and sigh in resignation. He opened his eyes again when the jockeying for position eased into smooth flight. He recognized the old home place by the contour of its sun panels, began to pull out credits to pay the driver as the aircar fell like a stone toward the driveway in front of his sister's house. His every impulse was to tell the driver to land at his parents' home. It was sheer fear that stifled that urge. An urgent is never sent lightly. Personal urgents were usually bad news. If that were true in this case, chances were good that the dire tidings concerned either his mother or his father. The others, Ruth, Sarah, Sheba, and brother Joshua were too young and vital to be ill or—worse.

"Have a nice one, Cap'n," the driver said as David handed him a generous tip. After selling his load of diamonds and emeralds in the Zede System he could afford to be generous. His years in the jewel trading business had made him a very rich man, but that last cargo represented a coup that would have impressed men far richer than he.

Ruth Webster checked him by viewer before she opened the door.

"Welcome home, David," she said. She made no offer to hug or be hugged, but her smile was warm. She was a woman at the peak of her feminine appeal, lithely built, slender, and shapely. Her hair matched David's in color, mouse brown, and their brown eyes were of a kind. It had often been said that the only way you could tell David and Ruth apart was that Ruth was smaller and prettier.

"Hi, Sis," he said. "Sorry I'm late."

"Come in," Ruth said.

Nothing had changed in Ruth Webster's house since the last time David had visited Tigian II. The carpets were thick enough to need mowing. The furniture was traditional, dark woods gleaming, rich fabrics blending their colors with the very good works of art which adorned the walls.

"I got your urgent when I arrived at T-Port," David said.

Ruth sat in a leather chair. She was dressed in a light blue sheath that showed her slender body to good advantage. "Do you care for something?" she asked, as she drew one shapely leg up under her.

"No, thanks."

"You're tired. Sit down."

"No," he said, smiling. She had always tended to think that she knew him better than he knew himself. "I'm not tired. Is your news so bad that I need to sit down?"

"I don't know," she said.

"Perhaps you'd better tell me then, and let me decide."

"Shortly after your last visit home Papa and Mama bought a Mule," Ruth said. Ruth was the only one of the five children that called their parents Papa and Mama.

"I'll be damned," he said, relieved. Dan Webster had never been a totally predictable man. Buying a space-going tug was just the sort of thing he might do. David laughed. "Was that why Dad wanted me to give him a quick course in space navigation last time I was here?"

"I don't know whether he had formed his plans completely by that time. He bought the ship about three months after you left. Sarah and I thought that they'd just use it to take little trips, like over to Xanthos, or to Terra II for camping and wilderness hiking and all those things that Papa talked about doing when he retired. Instead—"

David felt apprehensive again. Ruth was the rock of the family, always capable of handling any crisis without mussing her hair, and he could see that she was worried.

"—he provisioned the Mule for a long trek and started out down the *Rimfire*'s extragalactic routes—"

"Whee," David said.

"We had regular messages from them for a while. Mama would send them. She was very impressed by the distances. Each message was just about the same, something like, 'well, here we are two-thousand-three-hundred parsecs from home.'"

"And then?"

"We had not heard for more than six months when I sent the urgent to you."

"Over a year since you heard from them?"

She nodded.

"You notified X&A?"

"I called the Tigian office. Then Joshua arranged for X&A Headquarters on Xanthos to send out an all-beacons search bulletin."

"Nothing?"

"Nothing. An X&A patrol vessel crossed paths with them out beyond the periphery. The patrol ship was downrange when Mama sent her last message, so they noted *Old Folks'* position in their log."

"Do you have those position coordinates?"

"Joshua does."

"Where's old Josh now?"

"He's doing a stint of administrative duty on Xanthos."

"Serves him right," David chuckled.

"X&A says not to worry. It looks as if *Old Folks* left the established routes right after Mama's last message. Joshua says that he'll have a patrol take a look in-galaxy from that point next time one is passing."

"Sounds as if Josh isn't too worried."

"I am. And so is Sarah."

"Well, Sarah would be."

"Now, David."

David smiled wryly. "How are Sarah and all the brood?" Sarah had married well, at least by her standards, plucking a plum out of the T-Town social circle, a gold-plated plum that gave her a ten bedroom town house and country homes in all of the right spots. Happy as a grasping little woman could be, she had immediately started producing offspring so that her rich husband would have heirs.

"She would like very much to see you," Ruth said.

"Let's get back to Josh. He doesn't seem to be too worried?"

"He says that if Papa were really intent on doing some planet prospecting he could spend every month of the three years for which he had provisions laying down blink routes out there in the unexplored areas. He says there'd be no communications because the temporary beacons a small ship carries don't pass blink signals."

"Right. The tug was provisioned for three years?"

"With a store of condensed space rations sufficient for another year of rather boring eating."

"Hummm. So they've got decent food for another fourteen months and reserves to spare."

"David, I don't want to say it, hate to think it—"

"I'll go out there," David said.

"Thank you."

"Hey," he said, "they're my parents, too."

"I knew you'd do something."

"I think if Joshua thought it necessary he'd have already done something," David said.

"You know Joshua. He can get pretty well self-involved. Right now his biggest concern is getting good ratings from his superiors. He says that a tour of administrative duties at headquarters is a prerequisite for promotion to captain."

"I think you might be doing old Josh a disservice, thinking like that."

Ruth shrugged. "You haven't asked about our little sister."

"Haven't had a chance," David said. "How is the Queen?"

"She's on a frontier planet in toward the core filming still another version of the Legend of Miaree,'' Ruth said, smiling fondly. "She has the lead."

"Oh, Lord, Sheba with wings?"

"She'll be cute."

"She is always cute," David said, remembering his youngest sister with fondness. "So she doesn't know about this?"

"There's nothing she could do," Ruth said. "I thought it best to let her finish her work before telling her. By that time maybe we'll know what—" She paused as the door chimes announced an arrival.

It was the delivery from the men's store. David explained to Ruth what it was all about as he gave the delivery boy his card and watched as the charge was recorded. When the boy was gone, he said, "Just put these things on a top shelf somewhere until the next time I visit."

"If you weren't going to use them, why didn't you send them back?"

He shrugged. It would have been difficult to explain to Ruth that the few hundred credits involved meant nothing to him. Ruth, the serious one in the family, had majored in basic education. To a schoolteacher a few hundred credits meant something. Ruth had never married. Her job was her life, the children she taught her family. More than once David, as her twin, had brought up the subject of marriage only to be told fondly but firmly that, one, the right man had not come along, and, two, that she had no desire to be married in the first place. Although it was against his morality and everything that Fran Webster had taught her children, David hoped that now and then a gentleman caller sneaked into Ruth's pristine bed. She was simply too much woman to be wasted. He loved all of his siblings, even Sarah, but his twin sister was special and he wanted her to have everything that life had to offer. It made him angry when he offered to do things such as buy her a larger and more luxurious home only to be refused. She was her own woman, content to live on her teacher's income, reserved, sometimes distant, perhaps just a bit warped by her years of living alone. It embarrassed her for him to kiss her on the cheek when saying good-bye or hello after a long absence. She had accepted his gift of a sporty little aircar with some reluctance; she walked back and forth to her school, took the aircar out only on special occasions.

He watched as she placed his purchases carefully on a table.

"Will you leave soon?" she asked.

"The sooner the better," he said. "The sooner I leave the sooner you'll be relieved of your worry."

"May I go with you?" She asked the question in a small voice, as if afraid that he would refuse.

"Of course," he said.

She looked stricken.

"Hey, if you don't want to go—"

"I do, really. It's just that I didn't expect such instant agreement to my request. You'll have to tell me what to pack."

"Pack as if you were going to spend a year in the house with all the doors and windows permanently locked. That means you won't need too much clothing. The ship's stores will have all of the toilet articles. She's state-of-the-art, a rich man's toy, so there's even a good selection of cosmetics and perfumes and a supply of one-piece disposable jumpsuits in a variety of colors.''

"Like the women wear on X&A ships?"

"Yep."

"A bit too revealing for me."

"Comfortable, though." He grinned. "Actually, bring along whatever you want to bring. There's lots of room. Ship's laundry will handle washing and ironing."

"Some books? A few films?"

"You won't need any entertainment material unless it's something so esoteric it isn't found in the Library of the Confederation."

She nodded. "Yes. I forgot the capacity of the new computers. Yes, I suppose that will be enough."

He laughed. A person would have to live multiples of the average six-score life span to read and view the millions of volumes and films that were stored in the *Fran Webster*'s entertainment banks.

"Tomorrow morning too soon?" he asked.

She paled, bit her lip. "I guess I can call my superintendent tonight."

"Take more time if you need it."

"Thank you," she said. "Perhaps another day?"

CHAPTER THREE

Commander Joshua Webster was out of uniform when the door chimes began to demand that he divert his attention away from the sleek, feminine curves of the lovely young lieutenant who was also in a total state of undress. His first thought was to ignore the musical clamor.

"Josh," the lieutenant complained, "I really can't concentrate with all that noise."

"They'll give up in a few seconds," Josh said, as he let his lips scale a luscious, small, darkly pointed mountain.

"Josh," she protested, pushing at him.

"All right, damn it," he said. He stood beside the bed for a moment, smiling down at her. He was a tautly built man, lean of waist, with the long, smooth muscles that spoke of good but not fanatic physical conditioning. "Don't go away."

She let her eyes fall to his narrow hips, his manhood. "Not a chance."

Josh slipped into a silk-smooth dressing gown, brushed his blond hair back with his fingers as he glanced into a mirror, and padded barefoot to the entrance.

"Oh, no," he said, as he looked into the matched faces of his twin siblings.

"I do like these loving, enthusiastic, familial greetings," David Webster said.

"I think that we may have come at a bad time," Ruth said, smiling ingenuously at Joshua. "Did we interrupt something, Brother Joshua?"

"You could say that," Josh admitted sheepishly.

"Well, we could come back later," David said.

"Fine, thanks, David," Josh said.

"But we won't." He pushed past Josh. He was the taller, and he was more powerfully built.

"Look," Josh said, "you know I'm pleased to see you, both of you, but—"

"We were hoping that you could put us up for the night," Ruth said. "You do still have a guest room?"

"Yes." Josh ran his hand through his hair. The golden hue of it made both real and simulated blonde ladies envious. He looked more like the younger sister, Sheba, than like Ruth and David. There were those who, looking at the five biblically named Webster offspring and not knowing the strictly conventional morality of the parents, speculated as to whether Dan and Fran were at home on the same nights when Josh and Sheba were conceived.

Josh spread his hands. "You wouldn't like to go out and have a bite to eat? On me? There's a good restaurant just around the corner."

"Thank you, we ate at the Port," David said.

"You're doing this deliberately," Josh said.

Ruth raised her eyebrows. "Doing what, little

brother? Are you trying to tell me that, heaven forbid, you have a—'' She gasped in mock shock. ''—girl in your bedroom?''

''Not any more,'' the lieutenant said as she came out of the room and slammed the door behind her. Her sprucely simple Service blue skirt was just a bit awry, her blouse not quite tucked in properly.

''Angela—'' Josh pleaded as he watched the lieutenant's stiff, straight back disappear toward the entry.

The lieutenant turned. Her smile showed that she was aptly named, for it was angelic. ''Family matters first,'' she said. ''Call me when you're free, Josh.'' She closed the door quietly behind her.

''Nice girl,'' Ruth said.

''Old Josh could always pick 'em,'' David said.

''I'm thinking of marrying this one,'' Josh said.

Ruth clutched at her heart. ''Easy,'' she said. ''I'm sensitive to shock.''

Josh pouted for a moment, then beamed. ''Well, hell, aside from the fact that you've ruined my evening, it's great to see you.''

''I guess you'll have to sleep on the couch,'' Ruth said to David.

''Unless little brother wants to be a good host and give me his bed,'' David said.

''You're here about Dad and Mother,'' Josh said.

Ruth's face softened. ''Any word?''

''None. I've been doing my best to change the schedule, but it's going to be at least another four months before a patrol vessel is in that sector.''

He sat down, pulled his dressing gown tight around him. "There's really no need to worry, Ruth. You know the old man. He's thorough. He's a nut for detail. My guess is that once he found himself in an unexplored sector with a few million likely stars to check out he started with the nearest one and began methodically to work his way in toward the core. David can tell you how time consuming that can be. They're out there somewhere having the time of their lives, a second honeymoon. You know how we all used to be just a little jealous of their closeness. If ever a couple made a completion, just the two of them together, it's Dad and Mom. They've just sorta lost track of time, I'd guess. When they have to start eating space rations, they'll come out a lot faster than they went in."

"I want you to be right," David said.

"Yes," Ruth said, nodding.

"But?" Josh asked.

"I've got a new Zede Starliner that needs a shakedown cruise," David said, "and good company for the trip."

"You must be concerned, to leave your job and your precious kiddies," Josh said to Ruth.

She nodded again.

"We'll need the coordinates for the point where they left the extragalactic route," David said.

Josh nodded. "A Zede Starliner? C or D series?"

"E," David said.

Josh whistled. "Is what you do legal?"

"Why?" David asked. "Thinking of coming in with me?"

"Actually," Josh said, "the Service would suffer greatly if I left." But, he was thinking, even if he made admiral some day, even if he made fleet admiral, which was highly unlikely since the last three had been Far Seers from Old Earth, he'd never be able to afford an E series Starliner.

"I'm a little bit tired," Ruth said.

Josh showed her the guest room and the facilities. David poured himself a glass of Selbelese wine, the finest in the U.P. Josh came back into the room and sat down.

"Where did Dad take his orientation?" David asked.

"He took night courses at the academy in T-Town before he retired and then he spent three months in flight training."

"Three months."

"He's good," Josh said. "I checked him out when he and Mom came through here to get their permits. I wouldn't want to put him into a mock battle against young hotshots, but he's fully capable of taking that old Mule star-hopping out in the big empty."

David was feeling the warmth of the wine. The tension began to leave him. He liked his younger brother, enjoyed being with him. Josh's reassurances had the ring of truth.

"Wouldn't care to take leave and go with us?" David asked, after a comfortable silence.

"Dave, the promotion list comes up next month. I've been breaking my ass to make it." He spread his hands. "If I felt there was some real danger to Mom and Dad, I'd go in a heartbeat, but I want to get back into space, and I want to go back out there as H.M.F.I.C. of my own ship. I want those captain's stripes.''

"Well, I think this family needs one genuine Service M.F.,'' David said.

Josh laughed. ''The Webster kids haven't done too badly, have they?''

"One Service captain-to-be on the way up, a famous holostar, a dedicated education professional—''

"A businessman rich enough to own a Starliner and—''

David made a face. ''One social lioness.''

"Not bad,'' Josh grinned. ''Not even the lioness. I know that Mom and Dad are proud. They told me so when they were here. Got right mushy about it. Mom acted as if she was leaving forever instead of—''

He paused, his face going pale. He had forgotten how sentimental his mother had been on that last night.

David asked, ''Mother had a bad feeling about the trip?''

Josh told himself that he was being foolish. ''You know Mom. She cries when Sarah and her kids leave to go home—all the way across town.''

David laughed. He always told his mother goodbye in the house and hurried away lest she follow him out to the aircar and make his own eyes misty by her weeping.

"Show me that couch,'' he said. ''We're scheduled for an early lift-off.''

"I'll wake you at five.''

"Not that early,'' David said.

"There's something I need to arrange before you leave," Josh said. "It might take some time."

True to his word, Josh was up before sunrise. A blast of music so accurately reproduced that one could almost reach out and touch the musicians brought Ruth out of a dreamless sleep instantly. David was not far behind. They had breakfast at Josh's favorite neighborhood restaurant and joined a stream of centrally directed aircar traffic in Josh's little runabout. At the huge X&A headquarters complex Josh left the aircar in the care of an attendant who would file it somewhere in a cavernous underground park with a few thousand other vehicles and escorted his brother and sister to his office. The lovely young lieutenant who had left Josh's apartment with her uniform in some disarray looked up from her desk and smiled brightly.

"Morning, sir," she said.

"Lieutenant," Josh said. "Meet my brother and sister, Ruth and David. Kids, this is my executive assistant, Lieutenant Angela."

"A pleasure," David said.

"We've met," Ruth said with evident disapproval in her voice.

Angela's smile did not change. "Coffee for all?"

"Thank you," Josh said. "And see if you can get us in to see the admiral first thing."

"Yes, sir."

As Angela left the room, her uniform not at all in disarray, David looked at Ruth and raised an eyebrow. "Meow," he said.

"I do not believe in double standards," Ruth said.

"I'm going to marry this one," Josh said.

The coffee was Selbelese. It seemed that most things that were good to drink came from one of the Selbel planets. The admiral would see Commander Webster and his guests in twenty minutes. That left time to have a second cup and for Josh to run over the day's schedule with his assistant.

Flux cars, moving at daunting speeds along rails through narrow corridors, carried them to the admiral's office. David was surprised and pleased when he saw the lettering on the door: Admiral Julie Roberts. Everyone knew of the woman who had followed Dean Richards as captain of the *Rimfire*.

Service discipline and an iron will had kept Julie Roberts slim and vital. Age had touched her gently, with silver in her hair, and by accentuating the spacer's lines at the corners of her eyes.

"Admiral," David said, taking Julie's outstretched hand, "believe me when I say this is an unexpected but very real pleasure."

Julie's smile was genuine. "You're not exactly unknown around X&A, Mr. Webster."

David glanced quickly at Josh, who shrugged.

"We keep track of certain cargoes, Mr. Webster," Julie said. "Precious stones among them. In that field you stand out."

Julie turned to take Ruth's hand as Josh completed the introductions. There was more coffee. Julie was more than willing to talk briefly about *Rimfire*'s circumnavigation of the galaxy. Then she questioned Ruth about her profession, expressed the opinion that the work Ruth was doing was of vital importance, looked at her watch.

"Admiral, you've been more than hospitable," Josh said, taking the cue. "We won't take up any more of your time, but there is one thing."

Julie was all Service again. "Yes, Commander?"

"David and Ruth are going to find my—our mother and father. Perhaps you recall that their ship has not been in contact—"

"Yes, I'm familiar with the case, Commander." Julie turned to David. "I envy you, going into deep space in a Starliner."

"I would like your authorization, Admiral," Josh said, "to have a Seeker installed on David's ship."

Julie touched her cheek with slim, well manicured fingers. "Yes, all right," she said.

Josh sighed, rose. "Thank you very much, Admiral."

"I shall remember meeting you with great pride," Ruth said.

"And I," said David.

"My pleasure," Julie answered.

In the flux car David took his eyes off the walls flashing past to look at Josh. "What was all that? What's a Seeker?"

"Ever look inside a ship's computer?"

"Yes, of course."

"See a little black box somewhere down at the heart of it?"

"The X&A bug," David said.

"A prejudiced term," Josh said.

"Yes, I know," David said.

"I don't," Ruth said.

"The bug," David said, "is required equipment for every vessel going into space. It monitors the computer, records every order, every move, every transaction, and, through the computer, keeps a record of generator operation, life-support systems, everything that goes on in a ship in space. Some people don't like it, say that it invades privacy."

"But accidents do happen," Josh said. "When they do, there's a complete record of what preceded almost any incident short of a ship falling into a sun. The bug is also motivation to keep spacers on the straight and narrow. There are some strict laws governing space travel, laws that are easy to break when a ship is light-years from nowhere alone in space. So the bug keeps an eye out for infractions, such as changing computer logs, blinking inside a planet's gravity well, things like that. Information recorded in the bug's unichamber can be and has been used as valid evidence in court. In short, it's a monitor of everything that goes on from the time a ship lifts off to the time it shuts down power to the computer, and when you shut down power to the computer you'd better be hard and safe on a pad."

"I've read about it," Ruth said.

"The bug does one other thing that isn't so well known," Josh said. "It sends out low frequency radio waves that can be detected by the gadget the admiral authorized for your ship, David. The Seeker. The transmitter is activated by any unusual event such as accident or loss of power."

"I can see that it would be useful, but quite

limited. For example, if Dad's ship had lost power, say, six months ago, the signal would have traveled only half a light-year. We'd have to be damned close in order to be able to pick it up.''

"True," Josh said. "It'll be up to you to get within range. If—and I don't accept the premise that something has happened to Dad's ship."

"If there hasn't been a problem, the bug doesn't transmit?" Ruth asked.

Josh nodded. "So you're probably going out there for nothing. You're going to have to guess at the route Dad took once he left the *Rimfire*'s beacons. The odds are millions to one that he'll come back to the blink beacons by a different route and you'll miss him entirely."

"It's a case of no news is good news, then," Ruth said. "If we don't hear a signal from the bug on *Old Folks*, we can assume that they're out there joyriding, that they're all right, happy as kids at dessert time."

In a matter of hours the Seeker was installed in the *Fran Webster*'s communications bank. The influence of a certain Space Service commander, exerted through his executive assistant, got the Starliner lift-off clearance ahead of others who had been waiting longer. The Zede-built liner attracted a lot of attention as she rose slowly and smoothly on flux, went into her assigned orbit, and then disappeared as David punched in the first blink.

Xanthos, the administration planet, was located near the center of the volume of space occupied by the worlds that composed the United Planets Confederation. Although not nearly as congested as the zones inward toward the core, past the Dead Worlds, Xanthosian space offered no long blinks until a ship had traveled several parsecs toward the rim. Time became an element in space travel when the blink generator was depleted of power and had to rest while gathering energy from the nearest star.

During those charging periods Ruth familiarized herself with the *Fran Webster* and was duly impressed by the luxurious fittings. She swam in the small pool in the gym, although she had to rationalize the fact that she was swimming in the ship's main supply of water. It seemed rather odd to think of drinking one's bathwater, and, to one not accustomed to shipboard life, even odder to realize that the water in which she swam, the water she splashed into her face each morning, the water she drank, had been recycled only God knew how many times.

She spent considerable time with her library monitor in her cabin, sampling the ship's inexhaustible supply of books and films. By giving the monitor an order she could bring up every film in which her sister Sheba had appeared. She discovered that David had programmed the computer to isolate Sheba's parts, which was helpful in the early films where Sheba's appearances were mere bits. It was fun to watch her little sister as she developed her acting skills. Sheba had always been strikingly beautiful with her long blonde hair, her emerald eyes, her perfect little nose, but it was glaringly evident that she had not always been a good actress.

There were long, comfortable hours of talk be-

tween brother and sister, too. Good wine. Good
food. Good music. First, they did the remember-
when thing, reliving their childhood, laughing
about tricks they had played on Josh or Sarah decades before. It had always been Ruth and David
allied against Josh and Sarah, with Sheba standing
aside in neutral territory, immune to the sibling
rivalry because of her beauty and her gentle, loving nature. No one played tricks on Sheba. Everyone protected Sheba.

"A queen from the first," David said, chuckling
fondly.

"The way that little girl could wrap people
around her finger she should have become a pol-
itician," Ruth said with fondness.

Jump. Jump. Jump. Rest. Recharge.

David gave Ruth basic lessons in ship's operation and navigation. When she was on watch,
Ruth's duty was mainly a matter of monitoring the
instruments and the computer.

"If you can tell when something is going
wrong, that's all you need to know," he told her.
"Then you call me."

Ruth's curiosity wasn't satisfied with that, of
course. She spent time studying the manuals and
impressed David anew with her ability to collect
and collate information.

It was a lovely trip. They hadn't spent time together in many years. They remembered, they
found that their taste in books and films was surprisingly alike, their politics straight down the
conservative line, their taste in wine and food
quite similar. It was difficult to get a good debate
going because they thought so much alike. The

only way David could get a rise out of his sister was to offer to make her life more comfortable, or more luxurious.

"Damn it, Ruth, I've got more money than I'll ever spend. Use it. Take a trip."

"I take one trip each year," she said.

"An excursion trip with a bunch of old maid schoolteachers."

"But that's what I am, an old maid schoolteacher."

"I'm sorry," he said.

"No reason to be. It has been my choice." She smiled, touched his hand. "Why have you never married?"

He shrugged. "I don't know. Because I never found a girl as pretty as Sheba?"

She laughed.

"Or you," he said. "Never found a woman I could talk to the way I talk to you."

She was thoughtful for a few moments. "Well, old Dave, you may have put your finger on it. I kept looking for a man like you back in my salad days when I was considering an alliance, marital or otherwise. Could it be that the Webster twins are slightly warped?" She asked the question wryly, but a memory had burned its way through a sheath of deliberate forgetfulness. She was fifteen and she'd just been kissed by a boy named John Form, a rather handsome boy who had put his tongue into her mouth. She'd gone to her brother in puzzlement, for at the time it seemed distasteful and rather unsanitary, that tonguey kiss.

"Well, that's the way it's done, Sis," David had said. "It's called deep kissing."

"I don't like it," she'd said. "Do you?"

He had grinned and winked.

"Uggh."

"Maybe John Form didn't know how to do it right," he had suggested. On impulse, he had pulled Ruth to him. "Let your lips part slightly." She had let her lips open. And a burst of sunlight glowed inside her as his mouth covered hers and his tongue sought hers and engendered response. She had tried to hide her shameful reaction and apparently she'd been successful. She'd said, "Well, that's about the way John did it."

David was talking. She picked up his teasing line of thought again as he said, "If so, it's your fault."

"Pooh."

"For being the way you are. Caring, thoughtful, wise—"

"Wise? My God, that makes me sound ancient."

"—rather nice looking—"

"You say that only because we look so much alike."

"Comfortable."

"Ah, that's it. You're just too damned lazy to court a woman."

He grinned. "Could be."

It was not, by any means, the only time their talk had approached what would have been flirtation had they not been brother and sister. Now, decades after he had demonstrated the art of deep kissing to her, she asked herself, "Does he realize? Did he, too, feel a sun burst inside him with that kiss when we were fifteen?"

The *Fran Webster* blinked back into normal space at a distance of parsecs from the nearest star. "Oh, my God," Ruth said, as she looked edge on at the Milky Way. "Oh, dear God, how beautiful."

The fiery heart of the galaxy was a dazzling globe of diamonds, the bulge of it protruding on either side of the disc, the thinner disc stretching on and back from the ship's position.

"Now I do envy you," she said. "For having seen this before."

"But I haven't," he said. "This is my first time outside the galaxy, too." He patted her on the shoulder. "No one I'd rather share it with."

"Thank you. Thank you for this."

"My pleasure."

"Can we just stay here for a while?"

"Sure. We have charge for another jump, but we can wait until the generator is full again."

She toyed with the optics, zooming in on the nearest stars so that she could appreciate the distance, then coming back, back, until once again the enthralling spectacle was spread out before her.

"Come along," David said.

"Where?"

"Out there," he said, pointing at the optic viewer.

"Yes. Yes," she whispered, thinking that he was merely being mystic, or poetic, but he took her hand and led her to the central lock, helped her climb into a shimmering E.V.A. suit. She shivered in anticipation and some fear as the inner hatch closed and she leapt convulsively when, with a wild hissing, the air evacuated from the lock and the other hatch opened to—space, darkness, cold that she could not feel but could imagine. She was incapable of movement. She made no effort to resist as David pulled her toward him, locked an umbilical to the suit and to his, stepped out into the void pulling her with him.

She screamed.

"That hurt my ears," he said, his voice perfectly reproduced by the suit's communicator.

"Take me in," she gasped, having difficulty breathing. They were drifting away from the ship, weightless. She felt helpless. She squirmed and reached out. The reaction to her sudden motion sent them spinning, together, to the end of the cords. They jerked to a stop.

"Ruth!"

His voice penetrated the haze of panic.

"I want you to look."

He turned her.

The galaxy was one vast, misty jewel over her head, hanging there, but not heavy, ethereal, so beautiful that she felt only awe, not fear.

She turned her head. The ship's hull was a metal wall behind her, seen dimly by the glow of the galaxy. Beyond was—nothing, a nothing so deep, so complete that she had to stare at it for a long, long time before she could see the dimmest little points of light, lights that were, she told herself, other galaxies as large as, larger, brighter than the glowing dream of beauty that hung over her head.

"My God, David."

"Yes."

"Still want to go in?"

"No, not just yet." She giggled. "I'm going to have to change clothes, but not yet." In her moments of sheer panic she had wet herself, but she felt no shame.

"You can feel it when you're out here," he said.

"That, sir, is exactly the kind of imprecise statement for which I would reprimand one of my students."

"Pardon me all to hell."

"But I understand exactly what you mean."

During a long silence she listened to her own breathing, her own heart pounding, let her eyes close partially to dim the glory of the massed stars.

"Time to go," David said.

"All right."

She matched his movements, pulling herself toward the ship along the thin cord that was all that prevented her from drifting away into the endlessness of the intergalactic void. Then they were in the lock and air was hissing in.

Out of the suit, she kissed him on the cheek. "I think that is the nicest gift anyone has ever given me," she said. "Thank you."

CHAPTER FOUR

The *Fran Webster* rested in solitude in a black sac seven parsecs inward from *Rimfire*'s extragalactic route, having left total emptiness at the point where Dan Webster's Mule had made a left turn over a year ago. David had checked the last inward pointing permanent beacon left by *Rimfire*, but no messages had been entered into the beacon's storage chambers. Now David sat on the control bridge with his feet propped up on the console, hands behind his head, staring at the optic viewer. A few widely spaced stars made faint dots in the blackness. Ahead, if he set the optics for maximum magnification, was the thickening glow of the dense areas far away, so far that measurements in thousands of parsecs were beyond the grasp of the mind.

Ruth came into the control room in a ship's unisuit, something that she'd sworn never to wear. The tailored shorts showed her long, smooth, pale legs. The loose top hinted at the tipped cone shape of her breasts. The garment was revealing, but comfortable. She was brushing her sable-brown hair and her eyes were swollen from sleep.

"Why didn't you wake me?"

"No hurry," David said. "We're still charging."

Ruth studied the viewscreen. "You think of the galaxy as being made up of billions of stars," she said, "and then when you see it it's all nothingness, dark, hollow nothingness."

Her comment made David realize that he'd been feeling a bit intimidated by the vast, barren spaces that spread away on all sides. He had taken readings on all of the visible stars and it was going to take weeks of feeling his way along with the optics to reach the nearest one because out here on the edge of nowhere there were no close stellar neighbors.

Ruth punched up coffee with cream, asked David if he wanted a cup, made it for him, and delivered it. A soft tone sounded and the computer messaged that the blink generator was now fully charged.

"All dressed up and no place to go," David said.

"There," Ruth said, pointing to a dim group of stars that were as bright as any on the viewscreen.

David raised an eyebrow in question.

"Ever go shopping with Mama?" She didn't wait for an answer. "Or to a museum? She always turned to the right. Rules of the road. Keep to the right. Slower traffic keep to the right. In a shop she'd turn to the right and make a circle to the left. Same way in a museum or a shopping mall."

"And what about Dad?"

"Remember how Mama always navigated for him when we were in the groundcar? She kept the maps in the passenger side storage. She watched for signs."

David laughed. "Mama," he said, imitating his father's tones of irritation, "my job is to watch out for the other idiots. Your job is to watch the signs and tell me when to turn."

"Right," Ruth said. "So they're sitting here beside the last blink beacon wondering which way to go, where to begin. The visible stars form sort of a crescent out there in front of them. The distances seem about the same."

"A few light-years difference between that little grouping off at ten o'clock low and those at three o'clock."

"So it's six of one and half a dozen of the other if your intent is to check them for planetary systems, right?"

"Right."

"There," Ruth said, pointing to the group of faint stars at three o'clock.

"There it shall be," David said, punching in orders for the ship's systems to look as far into the emptiness as possible. When the optics had verified that nothing solid blocked a straight line extending into the darkness for a few Tigian astronomical units the ship jumped and David initiated the search process again. The actual movement of the ship was instantaneous, the preparation was not, although it took several of the small jumps to deplete the generator of power.

David began to include the Seeker in the search pattern when the distance to the near star fell below one light-year. There was, of course, nothing to be detected. The first star in the grouping was a loner, barren. The next sun was over twenty light-years away, and that was a close grouping for the rim area. He went back to the routine of jump, search, charge, jump, search, jump.

They swam in the small pool together. In recent years the styles in feminine swimwear had trended again toward the skimpy. David determined that he had one hell-of-a-fine-shaped sister. He looked at her with appreciation for beauty, with pride because she was of his blood, with renewed curiosity as to why there didn't seem to be a single man on Tigian II with eyes to see and persistence to break through his sister's penchant for living alone.

If there hadn't been the underlying worry about his parents, David would have been content to jump, search, jump, charge for an indefinite period. Being a businessman, he'd never taken time for exploration, and it was rather exciting to take those baby-step jumps into unknown space, to see a star growing in brightness and size on the screen, and to wonder if this one had a family, if this one had spawned a water world. He didn't really need the money that would come to the discoverer of a habitable planet, but he wouldn't refuse it. It might be neat to have a world named for you. Webster. Hell of a name for a world. Imagine having to live on a world called that. "Well, I'm from Webster. It's out there in the rim worlds. No glow from the Milky Way at night. Dark as pitch when there's no moon."

When the *Fran Webster* was just over half a light-year from the star, the Seeker communicated to the computer that it was getting a signal. A gong rang softly, raising David's hair, for that warning gong was a demand from the computer for immediate attention. That particular gong could mean only something out of the ordinary and in space surprises were usually unpleasant. "By the way, David, we're about to crunch prow on into a drifting asteroid." Or, "Oh, it seems that we've developed a little leak in the hull and all of our atmosphere is bleeding off into the big empty." Or, "There's an urgent blink message coming in."

David and Ruth were eating when the gong gonged. Ruth's eyes went wide as David leapt into action, his face tense.

"I'll be damned," he said, after he'd taken a couple of seconds to assess the situation.

"David, please," Ruth said, "I have a low threshold of terror."

"It's them," he said. "They're close. The signal from their black box is quite strong."

"Thank God," she said, coming to stand beside him.

His fingers flew, giving commands to the computer. Minute analysis showed that the source of the signal was moving—or that it had been moving when the signal was being originated. For two hours the communications bank blinked and chuckled and determined that the source had been moving in an arc around the near star. Another minute measurement told David that the signal had been shaped by a solid mass in the background.

"Orbital path," David said, asking questions of the computer, nodding.

"Projecting the movement shows this." The computer displayed a diagram of a planetary body orbiting the sun. And then the signal disappeared.

"What happened?" Ruth asked, frightened.

"Don't know." He ordered a careful scan. Just over twelve hours later the signal came again. During the period of silence the source had moved along the predicted arc.

"They've landed," David said. "They're on a body that is orbiting the sun. The orbit is in the life zone area."

"Which means?"

"Life as we know it requires free water. Not water locked up in rock masses. Not water frozen permanently in ice or heated forever into steam. Free water. To have free water you have to have a temperature zone that is below boiling and above freezing. The life zone. That area where the energy put out by a planet's sun is confined to a very narrow range. If you have water, chances are you have free oxygen. You can have a lot of other stuff that prevents the planet from being habitable. The odds against having a planet at just the right position in relationship to its sun are literally astronomical, and then you multiple those odds to cover the possible—and very probable—existence of toxic gases and such. That's why a good world is the rarest and most valuable thing in the galaxy."

"Mama and Papa may have found a habitable planet?"

"Well, it's a little early to guess. We know that the ship is on an orbiting body—or was when this signal was sent."

"Yes, I have to keep reminding myself that we're listening to the past."

"We'll just have to move in and see what's going on."

From the time that they first detected the signal from the black box on *Old Folks* it lasted only seventy-two hours counting the time when the rotation of the body from which the signal originated halted their reception while the transmitter was carried to the opposite side of the planet. With each reemergence of the signal it weakened. It became undetectable at a time when the source was on the side of the body facing them, so it wasn't just a matter of the transmitter being carried behind the bulk of the planetary body again.

"Punch up the Seeker data Josh gave us," David ordered, as he searched for the signal.

"Got it," Ruth said.

"What does it say about the duration of the signal?"

Ruth read quickly, then summarized. "The atomic battery is good for at least twenty years. The box can withstand almost anything except being sucked down into a sun. It's shielded from heat and radiation."

"And, I assume, the cold of space wouldn't bother it."

"Apparently not," Ruth said after scanning. "I'd say that's taken for granted because they don't mention cold temperatures specifically. If a ship lost power and air, it would soon become as cold as space, so the box must have been built to operate under such conditions."

"Any clue as to why it would operate for a while and then stop?"

"Let me read it all again," she said. Then, after a few minutes. "No hint as to what might have happened, David. Whoever wrote this apparently believed that the box is almost indestructible."

"It's beginning to sound to me as if Dad just blinked off and away," David said.

"But something had to activate the signal," Ruth said.

"Maybe it was just a rough landing," David said.

"Once activated, the signal can be turned off only by an X&A technician."

"But if he bumped the ship in landing hard enough to set off the signal but not badly enough to do any real damage, it would seem to us that the signal had been turned off if and when he simply blinked away out of range." He sighed. "Well, we'll go have a look at Dad's planet, anyhow."

It was just a matter of covering the last few million miles as quickly as possible and putting the Starliner into the orbital path of what was, yes, a planet in the life zone of the G-class sun. It was getting pretty exciting.

"They've found the Garden of Eden and they decided to stay for a while," Ruth said, as the *Fran Webster* circled the sun on flux for a meeting with what she was beginning to think of as Papa's Planet.

"It would be like Dad" David said, "to ignore every directive sent down by X&A about landing on a new planet before it's checked out by X&A scientists.''

"Papa wouldn't take any chances he recognized as such, but what if you were flying low over a garden planet? Wouldn't you be tempted to think that nothing could be wrong with such a beautiful place? Wouldn't you be tempted to stretch the law just a little bit to go down and have a closer look?''

So it was, with the idea of a lush, blue and green, living planet having been planted in her imagination by her brother, that Ruth was at first puzzled, then frustrated by the bright, reflected light that showed the planet to be a gleaming ball of ice.

"Papa must have been so disappointed,'' she said, as David adjusted the optics to cut down on the glare and get higher magnification.

"I don't think they would have stayed around here long,'' David said.

"It makes me cold just to look at it,'' Ruth said.

The *Fran Webster* settled into a stable orbit. Since David had not as yet had the chance to use the ship's sensors and detection instruments he ran a quick scan on the ice world.

"Hey, now,'' he said, as the metallic readings nearly went off the scale. "There's metal everywhere. It's under the ice but definitely not too deep. I'm not a mining engineer, but if I'm reading these things right those have to be the richest ore fields yet to be discovered.''

"Maybe that's why Papa stayed here for a while.''

"Could be," David agreed. "I think we'd better go down and run a complete survey."

"Wouldn't that be a waste of time if Papa has already done it and filed his claim of discovery?" Ruth asked.

"If he had filed it, it would be on record."

"Oh, yes," she said. No such claim—no claim at all from Dan Webster—had been filed.

Flying at a few thousand feet over the gleaming surface of the ice, the ship screamed through a thin atmosphere. Instruments clicked and whirred. The ship flew herself. David was sitting in the command chair, watching the screens casually. His head jerked when the sensors zeroed in on a small mound of ice and gave off a sharper note of self-congratulation to indicate that they had found a particularly rich source of metal.

With a grunt, David took control, slowed the ship until she hovered on her flux drives. He did an infrared scan. Nothing. There was something about the shape of the ice mound that drew him. He lowered the ship until the *Fran Webster* stood on her flux drives a hundred feet above the ice.

The ice coating on the *Old Folks* was relatively thin. The heat of the flux drives sent clear water dripping, then flooding down the sides of the mound.

"Oh, David," Ruth gasped, as the metallic hide of a Mule began to show through, then the square, awkward shape and U.P. markings along with the name, *Old Folks*.

David landed the *Fran Webster* with her port air lock not a hundred feet from the entry port of the tug. At first he was not going to allow Ruth to accompany him, but he relented. After all, if something happened to him on the icy surface of the planet she had neither the skill nor the knowledge to get the ship into space and back to the U.P. He helped her get into her suit, checked the life-support system himself, suited up, led the way out into the almost nonexistent atmosphere. The cold was not the cold of space. Sunlight glared off the ice. The suit's instruments measured the same contrast in temperatures that one could expect to find on an airless moon, torrid in the sun, frigid in shade. By all rights the ice that covered the planet should melt and run rivers during the period of sun and refreeze at night.

David halted, pulled Ruth to a stop beside him.

"What?" she asked.

"Something's just a shade off center here," he said.

"I beg your pardon?"

"Something is not right. What is your suit conditioner doing?"

She was silent for a moment. "It's cooling."

"The sun is quite hot," he said. "But there's no melting. The water we melted down with the flux tubes is already refrozen."

"I don't understand," Ruth said.

"You are not alone." He turned, started back toward the Starliner.

"David, please," she begged. "We've got to know. We've got to find out."

He hesitated. They were a mere fifty feet from the *Old Folks*. He could see frost reforming on her hull. Worse, he could see the large rent in the metal where the interior water tanks had expanded

with deadly results. Every molecule of air in the
ship's atmosphere would have rushed out within
seconds.

"Ruth, honey, I think you'd better go on back.
I'll take a look."

"No," she said.

The *Old Folks'* entry hatch was closed. David
checked for power with the suit's instruments. The
ship was dead. He used a small bonding torch that
was built into the suit's right arm to cut away the
lock. The hatch resisted opening, creaked and
grated as he pulled, then shattered at the hinges,
the strong hull alloy turning into powder to fall to
the ice below. He also had to cut his way through
the inner lock door and then he was in the Mule's
lower area. The blink generator was dead. No
flicker of energy showed on the instruments. The
ship's atmosphere matched the thin one of the ice
world. There wasn't enough free oxygen to allow
a gnat to breathe.

He moved forward. A rime of frost covered everything, including an irregular heap of—something—
on the deck near the external tools control panel. He
started to step over, halted with one booted foot in
the air, felt his heart hammer, his gorge rise, for
through the coating of clear ice he saw a face, or what
was left of a face. The liquid inside the eyeballs had
frozen, shattering everything like glass. On the face
and neck blood veins had expanded with the cold,
thrusting cords of red through splits in the gray, frozen skin.

"Stay back," he said, but it was too late. Ruth
was by his side looking down. Her cry was not a

scream of horror. It was almost soft, a hair-raising expression of grief that lanced through him.

Ruth knelt, touched the frozen forms. David knelt beside her.

Dan Webster had managed to get his arms around his wife and there they had stayed so that they were locked together in a glacial embrace.

Ruth was sobbing quietly. David said, "Well, they were together. They would have wanted to be together."

She turned her helmeted face to glare at him. "They would have wanted to live."

"Yes, of course." He looked around. Everything seemed to be in order. Aboard a ship there is a place for everything and everything had better be in its place if you wanted to have room to move. He left Ruth weeping beside the frozen corpses and walked into the control room. *Old Folks* was as dead as a ship could be. He used his gloved hand to wipe the rime off the covering of an instrument and the glass powdered under the pressure. Damned odd. And a lance of cold came through the insulated glove with painful intensity.

"What the hell?" he muttered. He walked back to the auxiliary control panel, lifted Ruth to her feet. "We're going."

"What about them?"

"Something's very wrong here, Ruth. We're going. We're going to go back to the *Fran Webster* and then we're going to get the hell out of here."

"What about them?" she repeated, desperation in her voice.

"Ruth, they're not going anywhere."

"We can't just leave them here."

"Come on."

"No," she said, jerking away. She fell against the control panel. Glass and metals powdered. He had to catch her to keep her from falling through the once solid panel.

"What?" she asked, her eyes wide.

"Let's go."

She made no further objection, followed him into the sun. Her feet were cold. Where she had touched the bodies of her mother and father with her gloved hands the flesh felt numb, painfully cold. She was shivering when David helped her strip out of the suit.

"You were quite worried over there," she said.

"Damned right."

"What killed them?"

"The cold."

"The sun is hot. It made the suit coolers work."

"Tell me about it," he said, placing his suit on the rack carefully. He moved swiftly to the control room, activated the ship's flux drive, started to push the button that would have sent the *Fran Webster* soaring away from the planet's icy grip. Ruth's appearance on the bridge stopped him. The transformation was instantaneous. Hot lances of overwhelming desire brought him to his feet. He could no longer remember who or where he was, or what he had been about to do. She moved to meet his lunge and they were together, lips hot and wet and hungry. He lifted her and carried her, a soft, hot, lovely burden, to his quarters and the big bed, peeled away the unisuit. He was aware only of need, a need so vast, so consuming that there was room for nothing else in his consciousness. It was not sister and brother who coupled, gasping, clutching, moaning in extreme passion, but two sexual animals from whose minds all else had been sucked away.

CHAPTER FIVE

Delicate, transparent angel sails extended backward from her shoulders. Her body was humanoid, and shapely. Wing muscles wrapped around her torso, giving the impression of breasts under a filmy garment that took its color from the short, sable fur that covered her. She was as beautiful as a butterfly with her regal stance, her protruding, multifaceted eyes, her delicate face and nose. She stood alone in an alien forest of shifting, whispering, oddly shaped trees.

"Goddamnit, Frank," she called out, "I'm going to break a leg in here. I can't see a damned thing through these freaking bug eyes."

Frank, the director of the largest and biggest ever production of *The Legend of Miaree*, sighed wearily.

"Frank, I'm an actress, not one of those Old Earth seers who doesn't need eyes," the whimsically delightful female said. "I'm supposed to be contemplating the possible destruction of my world, of everything that I know and love. I'm supposed to be helplessly enthralled by the maleness of a man from Delan, the constellation of the mythical beast. I'm supposed to smell like flowers because I've got the hots and all I can do is stumble over my feet because I see six of everything through these motherless bug eyes.''

"All right, everybody," Frank said, "take five." He pointed a long-nailed finger at a technician. "You, Big Brain," he shouted. "It's costing just over four thousand credits per minute whether this crew is working or not. If we were paying you enough, I'd take this lost time out of your salary."

"I wouldn't turn down a raise." The speaker was young, tall, and he was often mistaken by visitors for one of the holostars in the expedition that had come to a frontier planet whose distance from U.P. center was measured in parsecs of four figures.

"Don't give me lip," the director said. "Just do something about those Goddamned bug eyes."

The young man made his way carefully onto the artfully forested holostage, approached the winged female. "I'm sorry, Miss Webster," he said. "Let me have a look."

He put his face close to hers. His heart pounded as he was submerged in the sweet scent of her breath.

"Sorry, Vinn," she said. "The eyes always worked before. Something just went wrong."

The perfection of her form was evident through the skintight garment that simulated the Artunee fur of the alien female, Miaree. The protruding eyes could not hide the classic symmetry of her face. Vinn Stern had never seen a woman who was as nearly ideal as Sheba Webster. He was grateful for the opportunity to be near her. Every day he thanked his lucky stars that he'd stumbled into his job as scientific adviser to the producer of *Miaree*.

"Well, that's it," he said after having stood very, very close to Sheba Webster for a full half-minute although he had seen the reason for her difficulty immediately.

"Perhaps, Mr. Stern," the director said impatiently, "you will see fit, sometime today, to tell us what *it* is."

"Makeup put the eyes on upside down," Vinn said.

"Oh, hell," Frank said. He made his way through Vinn Stern's version of a grove of Artunee pleele trees. "Can't you manage to do the scene, darling, without having to redo the eyes?"

"Frank," Sheba said patiently, "I'm supposed to be an alien female. I'm supposed to cease being Sheba Webster and become a being that metamorphosizes from some horrid sluglike leaf-eating creature into a sensitive entity. I'm encapsulated in fur. I'm sweating my buns off. This stuff makes me itch all over, and I'm supposed to be able to feel love for some macho alien male? I'm supposed to be able to project that I'm a lovely, doomed butterfly when I risk breaking a leg each time I move?"

Frank sighed again. It took well over an hour for makeup to prepare Sheba's face and hair. He turned away, lifted his arms toward heaven in supplication. "All right, everybody, power down. We'll have an early lunch. Back on the set ready to shoot at one-thirty." He turned to Sheba. "Okay?"

"Okay," she said. "You're so very considerate, Frank. It's a genuine pleasure to work with you." The tone of her voice indicated exactly the opposite meaning. She lifted her hands and tugged at the bug eyes.

"No, don't, please," Vinn said, putting his hands atop hers. "Let me do it."

The sable smoothness of the fur garment was sensuous, the knowledge that it was *her* hands under the fur caused him to take a deep breath. He sprayed a neutrally balanced enzyme dissolver around the multifaceted artificial organs and caught them as they fell. Sheba's own huge emerald eyes teared from the residue of the spray. He produced a clean cloth, touched the corners of her eyes delicately.

"Thank you, Vinn," she said.

"You'd better go along with her, Stern," the director ordered as Sheba swayed away through the pleele trees. "Be sure they do it right this time."

Vinn caught up with Sheba as she stepped off the holostage. "I've been told to supervise makeup," he said.

"Good for you." She turned aside, headed toward a cubicle that had her name on the door.

"Ah, that's not the way to makeup, Miss Webster," Vinn said.

"Come in, I'll need your help," she said.

Sheba's dressing room smelled of girl—perfumes and powders. She stopped just inside the door. "The zipper is just under here." She lifted her long blonde hair away from her neck.

"Miss Webster, I don't think there's time," he protested.

"I'm being slowly boiled," she said. "The zipper, please."

He pulled the tab.

"We have to be very careful of the wings," he said. The zipper made a tiny noise. Girl skin emerged from under the fur. His fingers pulled the tab down the ridge of her spine, over the outward flow of her rump.

"Thank you," she said. She skinned out of the fur and bent over a wash basin to splash cooling water into her face, thereby destroying an hour's work in the makeup room. Her position emphasized the womanly outthrust of hip, the taut roundness of buttock. She wore only the briefest of undergarments. She was so beautiful that Vinn had trouble breathing.

"Would you please hand me the robe hanging behind the door?"

She turned her back to him and lifted her arms. He held the robe for her. She shrugged to nestle it on her shoulders and turned to face him. "If I invite you to lunch, would you be kind enough to fetch it for us?"

"My pleasure," he said.

He was back quickly with two hotpacks. Sheba pulled a small table out from the wall and they sat facing each other. When the lids of the hotpacks were removed, delicious smells joined the feminine scents of the dressing room. Sheba said, "Ummm," and attacked the food hungrily. Vinn, fascinated, could only watch.

"If you're not going to eat your meat—" she

said, looking up at him with her green eyes. Her lips were glossy.

"No, no," he said. "If you want it—"

"Thank you," she said, spearing his filet with her fork. She smiled radiantly. "Don't let it bother you. You're not the first to be amazed by my metabolism."

"You do enjoy your food, don't you?"

"I was my mother's despair," she said. "She was always telling me that it wasn't ladylike to eat like an outworld mine worker."

"Well, you certainly don't have a weight problem."

"Never," she said. "I can eat my weight and not gain an ounce."

"You're fortunate."

"You're not going to eat anything?"

He flushed. She said nothing more. He was not the first young man to be stupefied by her beauty. She never could fully understand it, but she accepted it. In her mind she was just Sheba, the youngest Webster girl. She liked her body well enough because it was lithe and healthy and sturdy, because it was capable of doing fun things like rock climbing and soaring. After a period of trying to hide her developing body with baggy clothes and a slump of her shoulders when she was a teenager she had learned to be thankful that others found it pleasant to look at her. All of her life she had liked pleasing people and she had developed that skill into a precision art. She had only to walk into a room to be the center of attention. Her beauty and charisma had made a place for her in holofilms, and then she had accepted another challenge and had set out to learn the craft of the actor.

Now, in the full bloom of womanhood, she stood at the pinnacle of her profession, ranked among the top dozen performers, male and female, who were familiar to viewers on hundreds of worlds. She had come to love the lifestyle that was made possible by her looks and by an acting ability that had been developed carefully from nothing more than a small kernel of talent.

"How did you happen to end up out here in the wilderness?" she asked, in an effort to put Vinn more at ease.

"Just luck," he said. "I was working at the Verbolt works on Xanthos—"

"You're one of those?" she asked, widening her eyes.

"Big brain, that's me," he said with a self-conscious laugh.

She was vaguely aware that Vinn, in addition to his other duties, was charged with keeping the film unit's computer in operational order.

"I'm impressed," she said. "I barely managed to fake my way through computer proficiency in school. I could never understand how data can be stored on molecules of liquid." She smiled. "But you were telling me how you came to be a part of our merry company."

"My old computer logic professor at Xanthos University was offered the job of scientific adviser for this film of yours," he went on. "His health wouldn't permit his coming, so he recommended me. I have to confess that I gave the proposition every bit of two seconds thought before I said yes.''

"Didn't like it on Xanthos?"

"Yes and no," he said. "All my life I thought that there'd be nothing better than having my own laboratory with limitless access to equipment and funds. I *knew* that given the chance I could make giant strides in computer science.''

"And?"

"And I spent eleven years in my beautifully equipped lab at Verbolt and the only discovery I made was that everything had already been discovered.''

"Surely not.''

"That's what I told myself as a sop to my ego," he confessed. "I was always the bright one in my class, Miss Webster. I was always tops. I was the great hope of my family and my instructors and when it came right down to it I discovered that I was, as our friend Frank says, just a Big Brain. I have an excellent memory. I'm a quick study. And I don't think I've ever had an original thought in my life.''

"That's being rather hard on yourself. After all, you're young.''

"Thirty-five.''

"Young." She gave him her best smile. "Younger than I.''

"No.''

"Oh, yes," she said. "I'm quite ancient.''

"You're beautiful," he whispered.

"Thank you." She winked at him as she lifted a spoonful of a quite delicious pudding, spoke with her mouth full as she put down the spoon and dish. "And now, sir, I think you'd better help me get back into my butterfly suit."

It was necessary for him to adjust the small bulge of the fake wing muscles that blended into the mounds of her breasts. He felt the softness and the heat. For a moment she was irritated as she saw his hands tremble, but the moment passed. He was, after all, not to be blamed for being affected by the fortunate blending of genes that had made her—so one fan magazine had said—the peak product of a million years of selective evolution. She walked beside him. He carried Miaree's eyes carefully. Just before they reached the makeup cubicle he said, "I have the use of an aircar. Have you had a chance to see the desert wilderness from the air?"

"No."

"If you're care to—"

"I'd like that," she said.

"After work, then," he said. "If Frank knocks off in time to leave us some daylight. I can have a picnic packed."

"Wonderful," she said, with a radiant smile.

Inside, he watched as the makeup techs worked. He, himself, applied the enzyme glue to the eyes and positioned them.

"That's much better," Sheba said, looking out through only one facet.

* * *

Vinn powered down the generators, put the portable Century Series computer to bed. The film crew was scattering. A pickup groundball game was getting underway in a field that had been cleared for the landings of supply and transport vessels. From one of the living cubicles came the soaring strains of the triumphant movement from Selvin Mann's symphony, *The Ascent of Man.* The murmur of multiple strings hushed the avian songs from the surrounding forest. The sun, whiter and much more fierce than the kind, yellow sun of Xanthos, was still three standard hours high.

When Vinn knocked on the door of Sheba's quarters she called out, "It's open." He stepped into her smell. Like her dressing room her living area was in a state of charmingly feminine deshabille. The briefs she had worn under the Artunee fur made a filmy, pastel pile on the carpet. The shower was running and the door to the bath was open.

"I hope that's you, Vinn," she called out.

"It's me," he said.

"Come and hand me my towel."

He swallowed, walked into a new smell of steamy moistness and fragrant soaps. The shower stall was enclosed in frosted duraglass, but he could see her silhouette. He found the towel. The rushing jet of water ceased. A slim, tanned arm disappeared above the shower stall.

"I'll be quick," she said, as the door to the shower opened and she stepped out. Her long, blonde hair was tucked up into a shower cap. Her petite, molded body was covered totally with the towel. She removed the cap and shook out her hair. It fell in a cascade of shining brightness. Vinn stood, mesmerized.

She laughed. "If, sir, you would kindly step out into the other room so that I can get dressed?"

"Oh, sure," he said. "Sorry."

"I hope you remembered that food you promised," she called out to him. "I'm famished."

"Yes, I did."

She appeared in the doorway. She wore lime colored briefs and bra and heels that made her calves arch attractively. "We won't be doing any hiking, will we?"

He swallowed. "No."

"Oh, dear," she said, "I'll bet you didn't have any sisters."

"No. Why?"

"It's obvious that you're not used to seeing a lady being casual in her undress."

"No." He made an effort that surprised him. "But feel free—" He gulped. "I mean, well."

She laughed in delight. "You remind me of my brother, old Josh. He was always yelling at me to put on some decent clothing."

"I am not yelling."

She winked. "But you're blushing."

"And enjoying," he said.

She lifted her arms high, slipped into a simple little sheath dress that came to a point just above her knees.

"I am ready," she announced.

They were approaching the car park when the director hailed them.

"Where do you think you're going, Sheba?" Frank demanded.

"Sightseeing," Sheba said.

"Our insurance does not cover flight in private aircars," Frank said.

"Mine does," Sheba said.

"Sheba, I'm warning you," the director said.

"Frank, I have a commercial license," Vinn said. "That automatically makes the aircar a public carrier."

"You see, love," Sheba said, "there's nothing to worry about."

Inside the aircar, as she settled in and fastened the safety harness she asked, "Really?"

"Really what?"

"Are you really licensed?"

"Oh, yeah. Unlimited, as a matter of fact."

"Anywhere, anytime, any size vessel?"

"I think that's the way it reads."

"I'm impressed anew," she said. "When did you manage to find time to study and get the field experience for that?"

"Well, I got my private license when I was in secondary school. I picked up some navigation hours in college, on field trips. And then I signed on as third mate on a deep space miner for a two year hitch to finish out the required hours."

"How old *are* you?" she asked.

"Thirty-five."

"Buster, either you're stretching the truth or you were an early starter," she said, disarming the challenge with one of her finest smiles.

"I entered Xanthos U. at fourteen," he said, as he fed power into the flux drive of the aircar and lifted it smoothly up and away in a soaring arc.

The desert began no more than four hundred

miles from the location site. The jungle became thinner, was degraded into savanna bushland, and then, just beyond a tall, rocky range of mountains that stored any stray drop of moisture in eternal snows there was the harshness of aridity. Barren sands and jutting buttes and mesas gave up the glory of their brilliant colors to the setting sun. Vinn slowed the aircar, lowered until they were crawling along just above the rocky terrain. The colorful upthrusts of the landscape towered above them.

"So beautiful," Sheba whispered.

"Pick a spot. We'll land and have our picnic."

"There," she said, pointing to a parched, rocky mesa. "We should have a fine view."

With the sun low the heat of the desert diminished to the level of comfort. With the coming of twilight it would be quite chill. Sheba spread the cloth from the picnic basket, set out the goodies that Vinn had provided, led the way in diving into them with enthusiastic "Ummms" and other brilliant comments such as "ahhhh," and even, "good."

Vinn, too, found his appetite. The sun sank lower. Sheba shivered and Vinn leapt to his feet to drape a warm wrap around her shoulders. He was still on his feet when Sheba lifted her arm, pointed, and said, "Wow, look."

A blaze of fire was sweeping across the cloudless sky from east to west toward the setting sun. Sheba jumped up, pout her arm around Vinn's waist. It was over in a few seconds. The fiery object seemed to be coming directly toward them.

It flashed by overhead and the sonic boom jarred them, reverberated in the arid valley below.

"There's going to be one hell of an impact," Vinn whispered, but even as he spoke the object arced upward, drove toward the blue dome of sky, and disappeared.

"Some damned fool just burned off a few hundred thousand credits worth of insulation," Vinn said.

"Wow," Sheba said, her arm still around Vinn.

"Well, there's still dessert," Vinn said.

She ate the frozen delicacy slowly, licking the spoon with evident enjoyment. The sun was below the horizon but left a lingering farewell in the form of a blazing red sky. Sheba finished her dessert, sighed with satisfaction, snugged the shawl around her.

"Thank you," she said. "That sunset is the nicest gift I've had lately."

"It is I who should thank you," he said.

"Oh, well, if you want me to arrange another spectacular sunset for you, just let me know."

"For coming with me," he explained. He spread his hands. "I still can't believe it. Me, having a picnic with Sheba Webster. You and I have grown up together, but with you on the holo-screen. I saw you first when I was sixteen. I spent hours in the library searching out all the films in which you appeared, and I haven't missed one since."

She laughed. "Good Lord, you saw my early efforts and you still like me?"

"Your acting ability developed steadily. Your

beauty just ripened, piling flawlessness atop perfection.''

She watched the play of crimson fade on the horizon. "Vinn, I understand what you're saying. When you were watching me in three dimensions and glowing color in a holofilm I was—"

"Bigger than life, because I wanted to see you on the big theater screens, not in a small room."

"And untouchable," she went on. She reached across and placed the tips of four fingers on the back of his hand. "But that's just the work that I do. That three-dimensional image is not Sheba Webster, but what she does to earn her daily bread and keep things from being boring. She took his hand in both of hers and squeezed. "This is Sheba Webster. I'm just a woman. I'm real. I have headaches and if I eat unwisely or drink too much I have a bad stomach and my breath gets a bit rank. When the day's shooting is over, I go to my cubicle and I can feel loneliness just as deeply as anyone."

He cleared his throat.

"So don't try to make me something I'm not, some object of awe and worship. I'm human, just like you."

"You're put together better than most women, you'll have to admit that."

"Ummm," she said, still holding onto his hand. "I'm glad for that, because it makes me a rich woman and it makes you like me."

"I do, very much."

"Like me?"

"More than that."

"Well, let's not move too fast. Let's take it one step at a time."

"I've never wanted to kiss anyone so badly in my life," he said.

"That's a small step," she said, leaning toward him.

She closed her eyes as his lips touched hers. She had kissed and been kissed many times, on the stage and in real time. She had never been promiscuous. She was not one of those who, in order to achieve her goal, bartered herself to the rich and powerful. From the first she had made it clear to the moguls and powers of the industry that she was not an object of trade, that she was Sheba, and that was enough to earn her her rightful place. She was not virgin, of course. She'd even been married once. That experiment had ended so badly that for many years she had avoided intimate relationships. However, she was a sensual person. She could take delight in good food, good music, a well done drama, and she could, with the right man, be a bawdy, delightful wanton. She wasn't sure—not just yet—whether she wanted to lower her guard enough to let Vinn Stern into her life, but with his lips on hers there was a moment when her libido stirred.

She let him enclose her in his arms. In the chill of the evening his warmth was stimulating. She widened her kiss, felt the hard muscles of his back under her palms, heard her sister Ruth say, "Sheba, Sheba."

"Ummm," she said, slightly annoyed but not questioning.

"Sheba, listen," said her brother David.

"Sheba, we need you," Ruth said.

"Huh?" She pulled away from Vinn's kiss.

"What's wrong?" he asked.

"I don't know," she said.

The voices were still there, heard dimly in her mind, the words indistinct but imparting a disturbing sense of urgency. She shook her head, gave herself once more to Vinn's kiss and the voices clamored in her head, driving away all hints of pleasure and desire.

"That's one step," she whispered, as she pushed Vinn away.

"I want to see you again," he said.

"Every day, lover," she said, rising.

"And at night?"

"One step at a time," she repeated.

She kissed him lingeringly on the steps to her living cubicle and for a moment it seemed that the voices were back. Inside she undressed quickly, cleaned her teeth, climbed gratefully into her bed. They came to her in her dreams.

"Sheba, Sheba."

"We need you, Sheba."

"Please, please, Sheba."

"Sheba, Sheba, Sheba."

CHAPTER SIX

Lieutenant Angela Bardeen pinned the twin suns first on one of Joshua Webster's shoulders and then the other. Finished, she stepped back and gave him a snappy salute. They were alone in Josh's office. The newly opened letter confirming his promotion lay on his desk.

"Very becoming, sir," Angela said.

Josh stepped forward, lifted her from her feet in an embrace, and kissed her.

"I would have expected more reserve in a senior officer," she teased.

"Tonight we celebrate," he said. "We'll have dinner at that place you like so well."

She pouted. "You always said it was too expensive."

"We'll blow my first month's pay increase."

She placed her palm on his forehead. "Well, you're not feverish."

He spanked her playfully on the rounded rump. The light slap was simultaneous with a thundering explosion that knocked the wall pictures askew and caused a suspended model of an X&A battle cruiser to sway on its hanging.

"What the devil?" Josh yelped.

Angela was on the communicator immediately. She listened for a few moments. "Some clown buzzed headquarters at supersonic speed."

"Well, they'll have his balls," Josh said. "They did identify him, of course."

Angela frowned. "I'm afraid not."

"You're kidding me."

"Sorry, no."

"Someone busts through the busiest air lanes in the galaxy at speed, rattles the windows of X&A headquarters, and he wasn't identified? What the hell, was he invisible?"

Admiral Julie Roberts and the X&A brass had substantially the same question. Captain Josh Webster was directed to find the answer.

* * *

"Captain," said the shift supervisor at Port Xanthos Control, "it was almost as if the sonofabitch was invisible."

"He couldn't have been going that fast," Josh said, "not and keep his hull intact."

"It wasn't that he was going all that fast," the supervisor said. "We had him on screen for a few seconds, long enough to measure his velocity. The speed isn't what bothers me. Any ship with a half-way decent flux drive could manage the speed. The question is, how did he drive into and out of the atmosphere at that rate without ablating his hull." He turned to a table, lifted a holoflat, handed it to Josh. "The automatic equipment snapped thirty or forty exposures. This is typical."

The glowing blur of a fireball was centered in the picture. "Computer enhancement?" Josh asked.

The supervisor handed him another holoflat. The central image was fuzzy and shapeless, nothing more than a concentration of light.

"What's your guess?" Josh asked.

"Sir, I don't know. It would be comforting if I could say it was a meteor. But this thing seemed to materialize out of thin air. Tracking started less than fifty miles to the east at an altitude of a hundred and fifty thousand feet. The track arced down to pass headquarters at two thousand feet and then went vertical."

* * *

"Sit down, Captain," Admiral Julie Roberts said. Josh nodded, obeyed. The admiral looked at him expectantly. "Well?" she asked.

"There seemed to be a tendency to brush off the incident as an unexplained anomaly," Josh said.

"That just won't do, Captain," Julie said sharply.

Josh spread his hands. "Something was there, obviously, something with mass to create a sonic boom and make an image on the detector screens. Any vessel with a fairly modern flux drive could match the speed, but at the expense of burning away so much insulation that it would break up."

"Josh, the whole place is buzzing," the admiral said. "You wouldn't believe some of the speculation that is going on."

"I can imagine," Josh said.

"We're sitting at the bottom of the most tightly controlled air and approach space in the U.P.," Julie said. "The volume of traffic dictates not just one extra-atmospheric layer of control but three. At peak times there's often a hold of hours on a ship wanting to land on Xanthos, and with three layers of approach control in near space a rock the size of your fist couldn't get through into atmosphere undetected."

"Something did," Josh said grimly.

Julie placed delicate fingers alongside her chin and stared moodily out of a window. The galaxy was big. Although man had been in space for thousands of years, it was still largely unexplored. And beyond the scattered rim stars at the edge of the Milky Way the bleak void of extragalactic space began. On the colossal scale of the universe man's little galaxy was an insignificance. Man himself? He was a frail creature, made of ephemeral stuff. He blustered himself outward from his small worlds, going armed and apprehensive, for although he was alone there was daunting evidence that others had gone before him. She had seen the Dead Worlds plying their eternal orbits in the hard, radiative glare of the core mass. She had read the Miaree manuscript, the chilling account of the death of two races; and she had come into contact with Erin Kenner's world. Intelligent species had come and gone in the home galaxy and one could only guess about the billions of possibilities offered in other areas of the cosmos. And to all races known to man had come death. Devastation. Genocide.

The far-ranging ships of the Department of Exploration and Alien Search went armed. Man knew his own nature. Long ago he had loosed the nuclear thunderbolts on Old Earth; and in the Zede War he had shattered worlds. When he ventured into the nothingness of unexplored space he looked over his shoulder, for there was always, embedded in his mind, the dread of meeting something like himself, or something like the beings who had not only eradicated biological life from the Dead Worlds but had cooled the inner fires of the planets.

"Well, Josh," she said, finally, "was it an alien probe?"

Josh shrugged. "Makes you think, doesn't it, sir?"

"I don't think we'll be able to say definitely what it was, not with the data we have."

"I'm afraid not," Josh said.

She turned to him, smiled. "But it's not your job to investigate unexplained flying objects, Captain."

"Still, if there's anything I can do—"

"There is," she said, standing, reaching for a Service blue envelope that measured eight by ten inches. She walked around the desk and handed it to Josh, who had risen with her.

"Your new command, Captain," she said.

Josh grinned boyishly. He lifted the flap of the envelope and pulled the contents partially out, exposing the thick, blue silk paper of a ship's commission. His fingers trembled as he read the name, *Erin Kenner.*

"Admiral," he said, "I'm speechless." The

Erin Kenner was X&A's newest, a cruiser-explorer of the new Discoverer class. She was only the fourth of her type to come out of the yards on Eban's Forge. Named, as were her predecessors, for independent space explorers, she had the muscle and the reserves to go anywhere in the galaxy. She, and others in her class, were miniature *Rimfires*, equipped with state of the art detectors, armed with enough firepower to meet any known or imagined threat.

"A crew has been assigned," Julie said. "You may choose your own officers."

"Admiral, thank you," he said, extending his hand.

"Thanks are unnecessary," Julie said stiffly. "Your selection was based on merit." She smiled. "I envy you, Josh. There are times, sitting here at this damned desk, when I wish I were your age with twin suns on my shoulders, a good ship around me, and all of space before me."

"I'd gladly sail under your command, Admiral," Josh said.

"Go on," she said, "get the hell out of here."

"Yes, sir."

She walked with him to the door. "When you read your orders, you'll see that they leave you quite a bit of latitude."

He looked at her, waiting.

"Yes, I do envy you. You can choose to blink in any direction, into any one of millions of unexamined systems, but if you choose to take the *Erin Kenner* to a certain point on *Rimfire's* route and strike off into the interior, you'll be serving two purposes."

She was giving him not only permission to search for the two ships that had carried four members of his family into the unknown, she was indicating that she thought it was desirable.

"I'm grateful, Admiral," he said.

"Well, Josh, I can accept the unexplained disappearance of a gentleman amateur at space navigation, but when a man like your brother David goes unreported after blinking off into the same area I think it's time to try to find out why."

"Yes, sir, I feel the same way."

"To warn you to be careful would be insulting to your standing," she said.

"I don't mind at all," he said with a grin, "and you can be assured, Admiral, that I'll be very damned careful."

* * *

Josh did a little dance around his office, brandishing the ship's commission paper. Angela stood, arms crossed, her face serious, watching him.

"Why the sad face?" he asked.

"When will you leave?"

"That's not the right question."

"What do you mean?"

"The question is, when do *we* leave?"

Her face relaxed into a beaming smile. "We?"

"If you think you can hack a couple of years in space, Lieutenant."

"I can."

He winked. "Well, then, why aren't you packed?"

"Give me five minutes."

"There's one thing, Angela."

She was immediately apprehensive.

"The *Erin Kenner* is a small, tight ship. We'll be a part of a rather closely confined and varied group of people. You are familiar, I assume, with the rule of service decorum regarding male-female relationships aboard ship. On a big craft, where the crew numbers in the dozens or into three figures, there's a certain latitude. On a small ship one's personal life impacts more intimately on others. To avoid complications one sleeps in one's own bed."

She smiled. "Surely there will be times when—"

"You will not try to seduce the captain into improper behavior, wench."

"Well, I can stand it if you can," she said.

He took her into his arms, looked down at her face. "There is a solution to what would become, I fear, a matter of some frustration."

"Yes?"

"If a ship's captain and one of his officers are man and wife, their bed can be the same."

"That's a proposal?"

"Yes."

"And what if, in the future, our orders put us on different ships?"

"We'll face that when it comes," he said. "Will you marry me?"

"Oh, hell, I guess so," she said teasingly. "I hate sleeping alone."

As he was kissing her, a vivid image of his younger sister was so real in his mind that he opened his eyes, startled, wanting to reassure himself that it was Angela and not Sheba in his arms.

* * *

The *Erin Kenner* lay in her cradle, long and sleek, one hundred fifty feet of gleaming, silvery metal. One had to look closely to see the seams of air locks, of weapons bays and sensor ports. At her bow, high, twin viewports were open, protective covers rolled back into their slots in the hull. Like opposed eyes, the viewports gave the ship a pixieish personality. In space the ports would seldom be opened. The *Erin Kenner*'s eyes would be electronic and optic, for the fragile men and women who would be enclosed in her durametal hull needed the protection of her density against the cold and the radiations of open space.

The crew were lined up at attention along the length of the ship when Josh and Angela stepped down from an aircar to the brassy blare of a service band. Two junior officers, selected by Josh after a search of personnel records, had already joined the ship. One of them called the men to attention. Josh answered his salute and, with First Mate Angela Webster at his side, walked slowly past for a formal inspection. The second mate and the navigator were male. Of the ten-man crew five were female. Josh had examined the service records of each member, and he was pleased. The admiral had assigned only top personnel to the new ship.

"No speeches," he said, when the second mate bellowed out an order to the crew to stand at rest.

"None of us here is on his first cruise. You can expect from me that the *Erin Kenner* will be run by the book. I expect from you that you'll do your duties as efficiently as your records show that you have performed them in the past."

He looked up and down the row of young faces. "I know that you're curious about where we'll be blinking. We'll be following *Rimfire*'s extragalactic routes in a counterrotation direction to a point which the navigator will be happy to show you on the charts, and then we'll be laying new blink routes into the interior. Not incidentally, we will be trying to locate two private exploration vessels which have gone unreported in the area. First, however, while we get acquainted with Miss *Erin Kenner* and she with us, we'll have a little pleasure cruise a few parsecs toward the core. As you know, it's standard procedure to keep a ship's shakedown cruise on well traveled blink routes. Our destination will be one of the new wilderness planets in the Diomedes Sector. From there we will return to Eban's Forge for final provisioning and any needed repairs or alterations before going extragalactic."

For two days Josh directed his officers and crew in dry runs of ship's operation. Only when he was certain that each man knew his station and his duty did he activate the flux drive. The *Erin Kenner* lifted smoothly from her construction cradle. She wafted upward through atmosphere, accelerating, and then the black of space claimed her. There, in her element, with the latest model of blink generator humming smoothly, she lay poised while captain and crew ran dozens of final checks.

On an order from Josh the navigator engaged the drive. The ship blinked out of existence to materialize light-years away near a beacon marking the lanes toward the galactic core. For some time the routes were well traveled. As the mass of the core brightened on the optic viewers, as the big emptiness that was space became relatively more crowded, the blink beacons were closer together, the blink lanes less traveled. The last few jumps, before the *Erin Kenner* fluxed down to a newly constructed spaceport on the wilderness world where Sheba Webster's holofilm company was at work, were marked by temporary exploration beacons that had not yet been replaced by permanent fixtures.

CHAPTER SEVEN

Sarah Webster de Conde was a small-boned, petite woman. She wore her shoulder length hair in a ponytail because there simply were not enough hours in the day for visits to the salons. For everyday matters she favored a conservative but elegant simplicity of dress. For the monthly meeting of the Parents' Panel of the Tigian City Educational Oversight Board she had selected a classic little business suit in pale mauve Selbelese silk. When she was recognized by the chairman she stood, ran her hands over her small but shapely rump to make her skirt hang properly, donned her black-rimmed reading glasses and confidently stepped to the speaker's stand with the notes for her speech in her hand.

Her voice was strong, and so were her opinions. Her subject was the lack of discipline in the Tigian City school system. "I am Sarah de Conde," she began modestly, although she knew that everyone there was aware of her identity, and not just because her husband, Pete, was a member of the T-Town Board of Governors and a man of substance in the business community.

"I'm afraid that I'm as guilty as the rest of

you," she said, looking not at the members of the Board but at the parents and teachers in the audience. "We went to sleep, you and I, during the last election. Things had been going so well that we were lulled into complacency."

Several members of the Board were glaring at Sarah.

"The price of good government, at any level," Sarah said, "is eternal vigilance, and we neglected our duty. As a result the forces of liberal permissiveness are, once again, in control of our school system."

"Mrs. de Conde," said the chairman.

"I think, Mr. Chairman, that I have the floor," Sarah said.

"Yes, you do," the chairman said, "but I see no reason, Mrs. de Conde, for you to be abusive and to try deliberately to create ill feelings between the members of your Board and the parents."

"Mr. Chairman," Sarah said, her brown eyes snapping, her delicate chin jutting, "ill feeling already exists between the Board and the parents of Tiglan City, and it was not I who created it."

The parents in the audience applauded. Thus encouraged, Sarah stated her case. "The purpose of discipline," she explained, "is not punishment. Discipline is an expression of love. Discipline tells our children that we care. Young people require and desire guidance."

She spoke for half an hour, often interrupted by frenzied applause. She outlined a system of discipline that put the responsibility for disruptive behavior on the student perpetrator and that student's parents. She spoke heatedly but logically. At the end of her explanation of the system of control that she and the concerned parents present at the meeting were recommending, she made the announcement that she intended to register to run for the position on the Board occupied by the chairman. The applause followed her back to her seat.

* * *

Sarah didn't trust Central Control. Her big aircar carried, after all, precious cargo. She had the car's controls on manual. She sat at the wheel with her back straight, her head high. Petey and Cyd, her two youngest, were strapped securely into their seats behind her. Petey was teasing his sister about her ballet skirt. Sarah was thinking about the meeting of the Educational Oversight Board and wondering if she'd made the right decision in announcing her candidacy.

"Mom," Cyd said, "you'd better start slowing down."

She'd been about to pass the turn to the dance studio. She checked traffic, lowered the car to street level, hovered six inches off the ground while Cyd gathered her paraphernalia and ran into the studio.

Then it was twenty miles across town to Petey's Space Scout meeting. Before returning to the dance studio to pick up Cyd, she had just enough time to stop by the sporting good shop to pick up the camping equipment she'd ordered for her oldest daughter's excursion to Terra II at the end of the school term. She had to go all the way down to ground level in the parking garage before finding a space and that made her late at the studio. Cyd was standing outside, her long, young legs exposed to a chill breeze by the ballet skirt.

Frenc, the oldest, was at the dentist's office. Sarah was late there, too.

"Mother," Frenc complained, "I'm going to be late for my Explorers' meeting."

* * *

Everyone was at home but Pete when dinner was delivered by the airvan from Seven Worlds Cuisine. Sarah had a meeting of the Library Improvement Committee, so there'd been no time to cook. Neither she nor Pete wanted servants, although they could have afforded any number of them. Pete came in just as she was getting ready to leave.

"Dad," Frenc said, "Marcia wants me to spend the night, but—"

"Enough," Sarah said. "I have told you, Frenc, not on a school night."

"But—"

Pete de Conde patted his teenaged daughter on the shoulder. "You know the rules, love," he said.

Sarah pecked him on the cheek. "Gotta run."

"I hope this won't be a long meeting," he said.

"Shouldn't be."

But a couple of the old hardheads had their dander up because the more progressive members of the Improvement Committee wanted to increase the number of holofilm viewers in the library. The

argument continued for over an hour. It was after
ten when Sarah dropped the aircar swiftly from
the local airlane to the entrance of her garage,
entered on the fly, pushed the close and lock
switch that buttoned car and garage up for the
night while the flux engine was still revving down.
The two younger children were asleep, Cyd with
a stuffed Tigian tiger in her arms, Petey sprawled
half-under, half-out of his coverings. She kissed
them both on the forehead, adjusted Petey's cover,
stuck her head in Frenc's door after knocking.
Frenc was watching a music holo.

"Don't stay up too late," Sarah said.

"I won't."

"Good night."

"Night, Mom."

Pete was propped up on pillows, his briefcase
at his side spreading its contents over the bed.
"Hi," he said.

"You look so comfortable."

"How was the meeting?"

She shrugged tiredly. "Same old stuff."

"Coming to bed?"

She recognized the look in his eyes. Her first
response was negative, but then she smiled. "I
thought I'd have a quick bath."

"I like dirty girls," he said, grinning.

"I'll be quick."

He had cleared away his papers and his briefcase when she came out of the bath smelling of
scents and powders. When he threw back the sheet
to allow her to enter he was nude. She felt the
good, solid surge of her libido. They had been
married for twenty years, and every move was

familiar and comfortable. He was considerate of her needs. She accepted his attentions as her due, as something felicitous and pleasurable but not necessarily vital to her continued existence. She knew that he liked for her to make sounds of approval. Her little cry at the end was not faked, but had it not been for his need to know that she enjoyed it she would, by preference, have been silent. Then it was his turn and she did her duty with a glow of fondness and satisfaction. He was her husband, her man, the only man she'd ever known sexually. When, as he reached his completion and she felt his throbbings inside her she suddenly saw her brother David's face and felt, for one split second, a forbidden, sordid excitement, she made a face of total disgust, wiped the image from her mind, and held her husband close as he kissed her lightly on the neck and face.

As she freshened herself in the bathroom she wondered a bit about her mother and father. She didn't stay in touch with her siblings as closely as she should. When she'd last heard from Josh, there'd been no news of the elder Websters and Josh had said that David would be going out to look for them. Well, she thought, everything would turn out right in the end. Bad things didn't happen to Sarah Webster de Conde. Sarah Webster de Conde had a wonderful husband, a splendid home, and fine children. Her life was so full of a number of things that she had no time for negative events. Mom and Pop would turn up with some amusing tale of being lost in the stars.

Pete was still awake when she got into bed beside him. He pulled her to his side and caressed her. "You're pretty sexy for an old married woman," he said.

"You're not bad for a staid old businessman," she told him.

"Speaking of business—"

He often talked about his financial affairs with her. She put her head on his shoulder and waited.

"I bought planetwide distribution rights for your sister's new holofilm today."

She was surprised. He'd never been involved in the entertainment field. "Really? That's not exactly your field, is it?"

"It should be a sure thing, and very profitable," he said. "I don't know if you know just how big your little sister is in the holofilm industry."

"Well, I guess she's a good actress."

"And almost as sexy as you."

For a moment Sarah could see her sister, golden, glowing, the end result of a million years of human development. "Hah," she said.

"Not hah," he said. "I mean it. The Queen's a pretty little piece, but to me you're the most beautiful woman in the world."

She laughed. "Well, whatever it is you want, it's yours."

She was thinking about her schedule for the rest of the week when, once again, David Webster's face was in her mind's eye. Something was nagging at her. She shrugged mentally and got back to priorities. She needed to begin a round-robin series of visits to parents' organizations at all city schools to get her campaign for the Board underway. Petey had his groundball practice on Thursday and Cyd had an appointment at the dentist's office on Friday. In a few months, Frenc would be getting her provisional license and, although she would be unable to carry passengers, she could provide her own transportation. Pete had already selected a sporty little aircar for her. In the meantime, because of her increasingly heavy commitments, she might have to think about giving up being a leader for Cyd's Young Explorer Troop. As for those silly worries about family, she didn't have time. Nothing bad ever happened to Sarah Webster de Conde.

CHAPTER EIGHT

Vinn Stern was supervising the loading of delicate equipment aboard a chubby freighter when the *Erin Kenner* fluxed down with a flair of rather ostentatious ship handling. The sleek, new vessel came plummeting down, mushed to a stop a hundred feet above the raw earth of the field, and settled softly into the dust. Vinn allowed work to come to a halt while the stevedores admired the design of the new type of cruiser-explorer.

"Whoever's aboard her had one helluva ride," said a worker.

"The skipper was playing amusement park kiss-me-quick," Vinn said.

A lock opened and several people emerged from the *Erin Kenner*.

"Okay, fellows, let's get it done," Vinn said, turning away. The men went back to work.

In the artificial pleele forest the film company was shooting stock scenes of the background. The basic exposures would be combined with the work of special effects techs on Delos, home of United Holofilms, to show the ifflings, the first stage of the Artunee life-form, crawling among the pleele trees in search of succulent fruit.

Sheba was in her dressing room, makeup in place, ready to finish off one small scene when the call came. She was eager to leave the wilderness planet. She glanced at the clock, sighed. She had always enjoyed her work, and that had been true of the Miaree project until recent weeks when a restlessness had begun to grow in her. It wasn't so much that she wanted to get back to her home on Delos, although she thought often of the great house with its extensive grounds winding among small, crystal clear lakes. She simply wanted, needed, to be on the move. There was an urge in her to go. She dreamed of traveling lonely star lanes to places she'd never seen. Quite often her parents were in her dreams, and Josh and David and Ruth.

One of the director's assistants put her head in the door and said, "We'll be ready for you in five minutes, Miss Webster."

They were reshooting the scene where Miaree first stood face-to-face with the alien. He waited for her at the top of a flight of steps. After special effects finished, he would be standing among smooth-skinned, graceful changelings. In the initial shooting he was alone. Sheba walked up the steps, slim and regal. Her soft lips were fixed in a formal smile. The alien extended both hands in a gesture of friendship. He said, "You are indescribably beautiful."

"Cut," the director yelled. "And wrap."

A cheer went up. The location shooting was finished. Soon the ships would lift off for the civilized portions of the galaxy. The actor who was playing Rei, the Delanian alien, kissed Sheba on her furry cheek.

"It's been a fine vacation, Sheba," he said, "but I'm ready to have a decent meal and sleep in my own bed."

The director, differences forgotten for the moment, hugged Sheba and complimented her on her professionalism.

When Sheba walked off the sound stage, she saw Josh Webster standing with his hands behind his back, tall and striking in his Service blues, a very attractive female officer at his side.

"Hi, Queenie," Josh said.

"Josh! My God," Sheba cried, running to throw herself into his arms.

"Careful of the wings, darling," the director said. "We might have to use them again."

"This rather odd creature," Josh said to Angela, "is my sister. Sheba, say hello to my wife, Angela."

Sheba took both of Angela's hands in hers. "Wonderful," she said. "I know you're a super person to be able to convince this old reprobate to give up his bachelorhood." She turned to Josh. "What a perfectly lovely surprise."

"I heard that they were trying to turn my baby sister into a butterfly," Josh said.

"This butterfly is going to flutter off and change," she said. "Angela, if you want to come with me, you can freshen up while I get out of this fur. Old Josh, you may come, too, if you like."

"I'll wander around and take a look at the sets," Josh said.

"Give us half an hour," Sheba said.

In the dressing room, Angela helped Sheba skin out of the skintight Artunee fur. She was slightly uneasy as Sheba was revealed dressed only in briefs and a filmy bra, but Sheba seemed quite at ease. She pointed Angela toward the facilities and went to work removing the makeup from her eyes. Her face was clean and smooth when Angela came out.

"Josh was right," Angela said, "you're quite the most beautiful woman I've ever seen."

"Hey," Sheba said, "it takes one to know one. It's easy to see why my formerly fickle brother chose you."

"Hush," Angela said, "or you'll have me wondering if I should ask you to get me a part in a holofilm."

"The cameras would like you," Sheba said, and when Angela laughed, "really."

Sheba leapt to her feet, slipped into a shimmering shift, pushed her feet into designer heels. "Let's go find the handsome one and sort out some food."

"You could talk me into that," Angela said.

Vinn Stern was in the cafeteria. He waved at Sheba and she called him over to the table, introduced him to Josh and Angela, and asked him to join them. Angela nudged Josh, calling his attention to the way that Sheba looked at Vinn. Vinn expressed admiration for the *Erin Kenner*. Thus cued, Josh launched into a glowing paean of praise for the ship.

"Hey, we get the idea," Sheba said. "You love your ship. If I were Angela, I'd feel jealous."

"I'm afraid I'm guilty of the same fault," Angela said. "The ship's performance was flawless. We're both looking forward to taking her on big jumps into the far and away."

"Need a slightly used scientific adviser?" Vinn asked.

"We could use you, Vinn," Josh said, "but the ship's organizational chart doesn't call for one. One navigator doubles as science officer."

"How about civilian sisters?" Sheba asked.

"That would be frowned upon," Josh said.

"Discrimination," Sheba muttered. "You're going out to look for the *Old Folks,* and for David and Ruth, aren't you?"

"We're going to explore the sector of space that both ships entered when they left established blink routes," Josh said.

"I've been thinking about Mom and Dad a lot," Sheba said. "They're not dead, Josh."

Josh didn't speak immediately. "I hope not, Queenie." He forced a smile. "There are still plenty of provisions aboard their ship. They haven't even been forced to go into space rations yet."

"They're alive," Sheba insisted. "And David and Ruth, too."

The *Erin Kenner* stayed two days on the wilderness planet. Sheba and Vinn were given a grand tour of the ship. Angela and Sheba found time for some girl talk and established a warm friendship. Vinn was busy stowing the computers, cameras, and other sensitive equipment for the trip back to the studio. He had managed to get a berth on the most luxurious of the transport ships with

Sheba. The company's equipment was stowed aboard the freighters. The temporary living cubicles, too, were packed away in the holds of the ships and the company had moved to their berths aboard the transports. The environmental police were at work, carefully erasing all signs of the company's presence on the park planet.

Vinn and Sheba told Josh and Angela good-bye. Vinn left the three of them together and went back to his final check of the stowed equipment. A couple of hours later he stood outside the freighter and watched the *Erin Kenner* lift fluidly and disappear into the vault of blue. Within seconds a chunky freighter's flux drive hummed and she followed the more graceful ship into near space. By the time the freighter had attained orbit and the navigator was setting the generator for the first blink, the much quicker X&A ship was light-years away, making multiple jumps along well-charted blink routes before having to rest for recharging.

Vinn buttoned up the locks of the equipment ship, watched it float upward to begin the journey home, boarded his assigned transport.

"Where in blazes is Sheba?" the director demanded as he entered the lounge. "The captain is losing his mind."

"She came aboard at least three hours ago," Vinn said. "She said she was a bit tired. I imagine she's in her cabin."

"Do you think we're so stupid that we didn't check her cabin?" the director asked, lifting his hands in supplication to unknown deities.

Vinn went to Sheba's cabin. It was in perfect order, a condition which told him that Sheba had not spent much time there. He opened the closet. Her wardrobe was arrayed on racks. Her luggage was in place on the upper shelf. He turned to leave just as Sheba's secretary appeared in the open door.

"Have you found her?" Vinn asked.

"No," the secretary said.

"Well, you know Sheba. She probably decided that she wanted to have one last walk in the forest."

"I don't think so, Mr. Stern," the secretary said. "Her survival kit is missing."

Vinn raised his eyebrows in question.

"A small bag. It contains her makeup, toothbrush, sleeping pills, a change of lingerie. Things like that. Things that if you have you can get along without the bags containing clothes and the rest of it."

"You're sure?"

"And her jewelry, too. A small box that fits into the travel kit."

* * *

"This is probably the dumbest thing you ever did, Queenie," Sheba told herself in a whisper as she sneaked out of the transport's cargo lock and ducked around behind the landing struts. From a short distance the sound of a flux engine came, purring softly as a cargo vessel prepared for liftoff. She peered around the struts. The *Erin Kenner* sat with open locks. Airvans from local ship's chandlers were parked near the open ports and as Sheba watched a man carried a crate of fresh greens into the ship. She waited until the green-grocer's van lifted away and another supply van was being moved next to the cargo lock.

With her little survival kit in her hand she walked to the open lock and entered. A worker came in directly behind her with a crate of fruit on his shoulder. On a wilderness planet there were no automatic conveyors to make resupply of a ship effortless. In the small space inside the lock a man in Service blues was checking off the crates of vegetables and fruit as they were loaded into the ship's chefmaster where they would be processed and stored. She ducked through a hatch. She had memorized the layout of the ship during the tour that Josh and Angela had conducted.

She ran through a tiny corridor that passed the entrance to the generator room, opened another hatch, ducked into the ship's gym.

"This is the dumbest thing you've ever done," she told herself as she settled down into a hidden nook behind a treadmill. The ship's climate conditioner was being affected by the open locks. It was working just a bit too efficiently, making for a slight chill in the air of the gym. She removed a tightly folded thermal sheet from her travel bag and wrapped it around her. Soon she was comfortable. Still convinced that she was doing the dumbest thing she'd ever done, she dozed.

Movement woke her. The ship was soaring. She could hear the distant hum of the flux drive. Her stomach lurched as outward acceleration ceased and ship's gravity cut in. In a matter of minutes she felt the peculiar sliding sensation inside as the blink generator was activated and the *Erin Kenner* was vaulted into nonspace for eternal microseconds. After the third jump she put the thermal sheet back into the survival kit and helped herself to water from a dispenser near the gym's entry door. She was getting hungry. Twice more she felt the eerie internal slide of a blink and then the ship was at rest.

She could hear the whisper of the ventilation system, and from deep within the metal bulkheads of the gym a series of tiny clicks.

She sat on a weight lifting bench and checked her watch. It seemed that she'd been in the gym for ages, but only four hours had passed since the last jump. She didn't know how long it would take for the *Erin Kenner*'s generator to recharge, but she was getting not just hungry, but very damned hungry. She was preparing herself to open the door and exit the gym when the door opened and a husky young man in shorts stepped in, nodded at her, did a double take.

"And who might you be?" he asked.

"I'm an alien stowaway," she said.

"Nah," he said, grinning and shaking his head. "I saw you in *Let The Night Come.*"

"Actually," she said, giving him her brightest smile, "that was one of my favorite films."

"I think it was terrible to kill off that beautiful girl," he said.

"But that's what made the film so poignant."

"Yes, I suppose so." He chewed on his lower lip in thought. "Captain doesn't know you're aboard?"

"No."

"It's strictly against regulations, you know."

"I suspect so."

He grinned widely. "Wanta hide out in my cabin for a while?"

"That's generous of you, but I don't want to get you into trouble."

He nodded. "Yes, it was a bad idea. Exciting to think about, but a bad idea."

"I suppose you'd better notify old Josh that his baby sister is aboard."

"The movie people gave us some rushes of your new film. I loved the scene where you fall in love with the Delanian."

"Thank you."

"You're sure you want me to call the captain?"

"What do you think?"

He sighed, stepped to a panel, pushed buttons, said, "This is Barkley; would you please ask the captain to come to the gym?"

Josh was wearing ship's shorts and tunic. His head was bare.

"I found her, Captain," the crewman named Barkley said, "can I keep her?"

"After I run her through the recycler you can have her," Josh said. "Queenie, what the hell?" He looked at Barkley and said, "Thank you, Barkley."

"Yes, sir," Barkley said. "Anything I can do, sir?"

"Leave," Josh said.

"I was afraid of that," the crewman said, going out the door.

"You run a tight ship, Captain," Sheba said with a giggle.

"Damn it, Sheba."

"Something made me do it," she said, and the lightness was gone from her voice.

"Yes, sheer irresponsibility. Sheba, this is my first command. They gave me the newest and finest light ship in the fleet, and you're doing your best to see to it that not only do they take it away from me but take my captain's suns in the bargain."

"That bad, Josh?"

He shook his head, and a fond smile relaxed his face. "Why?"

She tried for lightness again. "It seemed like a good idea at the time." His face darkened. "I had to, Josh," she said quickly. "I knew that you were going to look for Mom and Dad and there was no way that this ship was going to go into space without me. I had to."

"And I have to make a detour and put you off on a U.P. world."

"No, Josh, please."

The door opened and Angela, slim and lovely in a ship's one-piece, halted, her mouth open. "Barkley told me, but I didn't believe it."

"She had to do it," Josh said. "Something made her do it."

"I know," Angela said seriously.

"What?" Josh demanded.

"Why did we come to the wilderness world, Josh?" Angela asked.

"We had to take the ship on a shakedown cruise along well traveled routes. I used that opportunity to come to visit my little sister. I was foolish enough to want to introduce my new bride to her."

"And that's all?" Angela asked. "There was no other reason for choosing the world where Sheba was working?"

"No," Josh said, but his voice lacked conviction.

"Sheba, why did you stow away on the *Erin Kenner*?" Angela asked.

"I had no other choice," Sheba said. "I knew that you and Josh were going to look for my family. Our family."

"Did you think that your presence aboard would be an asset, that it would be necessary for us to have you along in order to find your family?"

Sheba was thoughtful. "Something like that," she said.

"Your brother, David, looks somewhat like Josh, but he's more finely drawn, older, more dignified," Angela said.

"Thanks very much," Josh said.

"And he has a small scar over his left eye, high on the forehead."

"You've met David?" Sheba asked.

"Only briefly," Angela said, "and his hair hid the scar completely, yet I'm certain it's there."

"Angela," Josh said, "we've got a small problem on our hands."

"You dream about him," Sheba said.

"And you?"

"Yes, and about Josh, and about Mom and Dad and Ruth. There are times when they seem to be calling out to me, calling for help, and I don't know how to help them."

"How long has this been going on?" Josh

asked, suddenly very much interested in what Sheba was saying.

"Off and on for about six months, I'd say."

"Josh?" Angela asked, her lovely eyes wide.

"All right, yes," Josh said. "I dream of them, too."

"You were going to them," Sheba said. "I had to be with you. I had to be aboard this ship regardless of the consequences."

CHAPTER NINE

It didn't seem to matter to the crew members of the *Erin Kenner* that Captain Joshua Webster was breaking more than one ironclad service regulation by failing to take the ship to the nearest U.P. port to offload a civilian stowaway. At first the young men and women of the ship's complement were a bit awed by their passenger. Each of them had seen at least one holofilm starring Sheba Webster. From their teen years Sheba had been the epitome of feminine beauty and sophistication. When they discovered that the Queen was an outgoing person who laughed easily, who was not pretentious, who was genuinely interested in what they had to say they adopted her as one of their own.

Sheba had discovered when she was quite young that the art of her acting was based on her knowledge of people. Even as a child she had made friends easily and had shown an inordinate curiosity about the intimate feelings and reactions of others. She had learned that it is quite difficult for any human being to dislike someone who is genuinely interested in him and what he has to say. When she listened attentively to one of her new friends, asking suitable questions at just the right time to encourage the speaker to bare his innermost convictions and dreams, she was not being manipulative. She was not seeking gain for herself, although gain accrued in the form of knowledge of the inner workings of the human mind. She was genuinely interested in what others thought and felt.

She worked out in the gym with members of the crew, watched holofilms with them, and answered their questions regarding the techniques of the trade. She joined a group of crewwomen in a literary discussion group, although her knowledge of literature was limited to what she had read in university and those books that had been made into films. The navigation officer gave her informal lessons in star identification. A young crewman allowed her to beat him at handball.

Her presence had ceased to be a matter of discussion when the *Erin Kenner* blinked away from the sparely starred periphery of the Milky Way into the total void of intergalactic space and rested beside a *Rimfire* beacon to draw charge into the generator from the entire spread of the majestic, tilted spiral of the galaxy. Now the blinks were long, measured in parsecs. The *Rimfire* route skirted the outer spiral on the plane of the galactic disc. Each blink put a larger mass of stars and interstellar matter between the *Erin Kenner* and the U.P. worlds. The communication link with X&A headquarters on Xanthos became more and more attenuated, for the ship's regular reports of position traveled from blink beacon to blink beacon along the *Rimfire* route and then zigzagged inward through the scattered star fields toward Xanthos.

No space tugs were stationed along the outer circle. The last major incident requiring tug service for an X&A ship had involved *Rimfire*, herself, and was now nothing more than a part of history. The general attitude was that accidents didn't happen to a ship being operated under X&A procedures, but every spaceman knew deep in his heart that ships had disappeared and would disappear again. Ships were made of mechanical and electronic things. Mechanical and electronic things failed. On the traveled space lanes help was always near at hand. Private sector space tugs, eager to claim salvage rights or lifting fees from a ship in trouble, were always within a few blinks. But out there on the rim one saw only gleaming, white masses of stars when one looked back toward home and the nearest private Mule or fleet class tug was back *there,* hidden somewhere behind that mass of stellar fire.

It was a long way home. Since *Rimfire*'s epic voyage only a few explorers and prospectors had seen the scattered stars that lay before the *Erin Kenner* as she charged after several long blinks. On the control bridge Josh checked the charts, nodded.

"This is it," he said. "*Old Folks* left the route here. So did David's ship."

Angela studied the viewscreen. "Rather intimidating, isn't it? Just where do we start?"

"There," Sheba said, pointing to a small grouping of stars.

"Are we having another psychic moment?"

Josh asked. He made a wry face, for even as he tried to sound sarcastic he had a feeling that he had lived the moment before, that he had looked into space from that particular beacon.

"Ever go shopping with Mother?" Sheba asked.

Josh nodded. "She always turned right when she entered a shop, even the grocery store."

"She would have been checking the charts and the viewscreen," Sheba said, "just as she did when we were going somewhere in the aircar."

Josh frowned. He'd heard the same words before somewhere, sometime. He turned to the navigator. "Mr. Girard, please take the watch."

"Aye, sir," Girard said.

"You two with me," Josh said gruffly.

"Is that an order?" Sheba teased.

"Yes," he said.

"All right, growly bear," Sheba said.

The expression took him back to his youth, to a time when the Webster house was filled with life and activity. Five of them, David, Ruth, Sarah, himself, Sheba in that order; and his mother and father, always there in time of crisis, always ready with a word of advice or a bandage for a skinned knee, whichever need fit the moment.

"Don't be a growly bear, Josh," his mother would say if he were cranky.

But, damn it, the *Erin Kenner* was not the old Webster home in T-Town. She was a ship of the fleet. She was Service, X&A, and he was her captain and, by God, if he wanted to be a growly bear he was, after all, in command. In space he had dictatorial powers over every man and woman in the crew, and over his civilian passenger, whose presence aboard he was unable to explain, even to himself.

He led the two women into the captain's lounge, motioned them into leather chairs. "It's time we had a talk," he said gruffly.

"Lovely weather, isn't it?" Sheba said, winking at Angela.

"I'm serious, Queenie," he said.

"All right," Sheba said, putting her hands in her lap demurely.

"From the beginning, then," Josh said. "You said, Sheba, that you *had* to be aboard this ship. Why did you say that?"

Sheba shrugged eloquently. "I was just worried about Mom and Dad and Ruth and David."

"But you gave me the impression that getting aboard was a compulsion."

"Josh, are you asking if Sheba was experiencing what you, yourself, have called a psychic moment?" Angela asked.

Josh flushed. The study of psychic aberrations was as old as mankind. There were things that could not be explained easily, but in all of the thousands of years of human history, going all the way back to Old Earth before the Destruction, it had never been proven that there were such things as telepathy or a spirit world or any of the other things propounded by self-styled psychics.

"I think we have to talk about such a possibility," he said. "Both you and Sheba have dreamed of the missing members of the Webster family. That, in itself, is not remarkable. What made me curious is the similarity of the dreams."

"And you, Josh?" Sheba asked.

"All right," he said. "I'll confess that I've had some odd feelings. For example, just now when you suggested our entry point into the area we're going to explore by remembering how Mother entered a store or a mall or a park I heard Ruth's voice saying the same words."

"I was thinking of Ruth when I spoke," Sheba said.

"I can't explain it," Angela said, "but there's a certainty in my mind that Sheba is right in suggesting which star grouping to aim for. "It's as if I, too, heard Ruth speaking. I *saw* her."

"In my dreams they are calling for help," Sheba said. She looked at Josh questioningly. "The same with you?"

He shook his head. "No, I don't dream about them. And it isn't logical to be concerned about them. *Old Folks* has provisions for another eighteen months. David is an experienced spacer. I kept telling myself that and for a long time I wasn't worried at all, not until a few months after David and Ruth went out, then, suddenly, the situation began to nag at me and I spent a lot of time trying to figure out how to get out here myself."

He spread his hands. "Now we're here, and I've got my civilian sister with me. Going against regulations is not in the character of the man I thought I was. When I took the oath of loyalty to the United Planets government and pledged to honor the traditions of the Service, I meant what I said. I can almost believe that someone or something outside of me influenced me to bypass at least a score of planets where I could have put my stowaway in U.P. custody. I don't swallow that explanation, but I don't have any other."

"You did it because you love me," Sheba said, but added immediately, "sorry. Bad habit, being flippant all the time. No one in our family has ever shown any psychic talent. It's a bit frightening to think that all of us are somehow being contacted by other members of the family over incredible distances, but I am being called, Josh. I am being called. I don't know where we're going, but I think I'll know when we get there."

"Josh," Angela asked, "are you saying that this—well, let's use Sheba's description of it and say this call—do you think it was strong enough to overcome your sense of duty and prevent you from putting Sheba off on a U.P. world?"

"Several times I was on the verge of giving the order to change course," Josh said. "Each time something seemed to say, no, don't do that."

"We're going to find them, Josh," Sheba said, "and for some reason it's necessary that I be there when we do."

"You're scaring me, you two," Angela said. "From now on we're going to be very, very careful, and suspicious as hell."

* * *

Because of her superior optic equipment the *Erin Kenner* was able to examine the family of planets circling the G class star from a great distance. Josh blinked the ship directly into orbit around the second planet and the ship's detection instruments were activated. Kirsty Girard, the navigator and science officer, began to report to her attentive audience, which consisted of most of the ship's crew.

"In places the ice is several hundred feet thick. It's thinnest on the mountains. Those huge, flat areas are probably oceans. The planet is big enough to produce the gravity to hold an atmosphere, but most of the gases, hydrogen, oxygen, nitrogen, have been frozen into the ice along with the water vapor."

The navigator went on to give readings on the planet's period of rotation, her electromagnetic field, her density.

"Her core is hot," she said. "She's got heavy metals, and one helluva lot of rich metallic ore close to the surface. I'd guess, without having probed, that she'll be a miner's paradise."

"Dad would have recognized the possibility of mining here," Sheba said. "He'd have filed a claim of discovery."

"Which makes me wonder if we made the right turn," Josh said. "Because if he had found this planet, he'd have certainly filed a claim."

Josh had set the *Erin Kenner*'s orbit to cover all of the ice planet's surface, moving from pole to pole. Below them the surface was monotonously uniform. The ice shimmered and reflected light on the day side and sparkled back the image of the stars on the night side. Aside from the indications of large metallic deposits the planet offered nothing of interest. When the surface survey had been underway for four hours, Josh left the bridge and joined Angela and Sheba in the captain's lounge for the "midday" meal. Josh had taken his first bite when the lounge was filled with the eerie, hair-raising clangor of the ship's emergency alarm. He was out the door in one leap.

As he ran the few steps to the bridge, he felt the ship lurch. Kirsty Girard was at the controls, punching evasive maneuvers into the computer.

"We are under attack, Captain," the navigator said.

"Weapons control," said a crisp, businesslike voice. "Missiles have been fired. Six incoming. Vectors—"

"Shields up," Josh ordered.

A tingling sensation at the back of his neck told him that the computer had responded to the order.

"Weapons," Josh barked, "have you determined the origin of the missiles?"

"That is affirmative," Weapons said. "Viewscreen three, sir."

Josh lifted his head. On the screen, made small by distance, was a compact vessel with lines that were unfamiliar. The *Erin Kenner* lurched again, seeking more room to maneuver in near space.

"Generator ready?" Josh asked.

"Full charge, sir," said the voice of the chief engineer.

"Navigator, blink set?"

"Yes, sir," Kirsty Girard said.

If things got too hot, the *Erin Kenner* could simply disappear to safety a few light-years away.

"Missiles incoming," weapons said. "Range five miles."

"You may take counteraction when ready, Weapons," Josh said.

Angela took Kirsty Girard's place at the controls. The navigator went back to her station.

"Range to alien craft?" Josh asked.

"Twenty miles and closing," Weapons said.

"At ten miles try her with a disrupter," Josh ordered.

"Aye, sir," said Weapons. "Disrupter armed and ready. Counteraction underway."

"Give me a close-up of those missiles," Josh said to Kirsty.

At first they were just tiny dots on the screen. Girard fiddled with the optics and one of the missiles sprang into the forefront. It was sleek and deadly looking as if it had been designed to be fired in atmosphere and not in the vacuum of space. There were no markings visible. The warhead cone was rounded, streamlined. Suddenly the image of the missile was replaced by a flower of red fire, and in quick succession there were five other explosions. The screen was clear.

"Incoming missiles destroyed, sir," Weapons reported.

"Show me the ship," Josh said.

The navigator had the attacker on the big screen. Like the missiles she had fired, the ship seemed to have been designed for flight within an atmosphere. Her metal was dark and, as with the missiles, there were no markings visible.

"Weapons, sir. We have disrupter range."

"Hold on," Josh said. "Kirsty, what do you read?"

"You're not going to believe this, sir."

"Try me."

"My detectors say she's got a hydrogen fusion plant."

"Interesting," Josh said. "It's been almost a thousand years since fusion engines were in use." He looked at Angela. Her face was set as she gave her full attention to the controls. "All right, Weapons, let's see if we can cool this fellow's jets a bit."

On the screen a shimmer of orange fire engulfed the oncoming vessel. It lasted for only a split second.

"Kirsty?" Josh asked.

"She reads dead, sir," Kirsty said. "No electrical currents. The fusion reaction has ceased."

"Weapons, stand by for close approach. Tractor beam ready," Josh said.

Angela's tongue was in the corner of her mouth as she edged the *Erin Kenner* into proximity with the alien ship. A close up view told them nothing more about the attacker. There were no visible viewports, no locks, no apparent access to the smooth, squat hull.

"Got her," said Weapons. "Tractor beam in place."

"All right, Science Officer," Josh said, "she's all yours. Let's see what's inside. Weapons, lasers ready at all times, if you please. Don't wait for my order. If she so much as wiggles, open fire immediately."

"Lasers ready and on target, sir," said Weapons.

"I'm getting penetration, sir," Kirsty Girard said. "It's rather odd."

"How odd?" Josh asked.

"Sir, there are no spaces inside the ship."

"Explain," Josh said.

"The entire area of the interior is filled solidly. I was wondering how she could have a fusion engine in such a small hull. It's possible because there are no open areas, no space for crew."

"A drone?" Josh asked.

"Lots of complicated circuitry, sir. It's a good guess that she's remote controlled."

"Weapons?"

"The only empty spaces I can find are the size of the six missiles she fired," Kirsty said. "I get no reading of explosive warheads."

"Nuclear material?" Josh asked, thinking that it was logical, since the ship ran on fusion power, that she'd carry nukes.

"None, sir."

"All right," Josh said. "Weapons, you're still on full alert. Science, continue your probes. Let me know if you come up with anything else of interest. Hold where we are until we've examined this beast fully. When you're convinced that you know all of her secrets, let me know and we'll think about having a closer look."

In the lounge, Angela asked, "You're going out when Science finishes probing and testing?"

"I want to see what's inside her," Josh said.

"I'll go with you, of course," Angela said.

"It would be unwise to put both the ship's captain and the first mate at risk at the same time," he said.

"Yes," she said. "Sorry."

"Angel, it was a damned primitive and pitiful

attack,'' he said, as he pushed his hair back with one hand. ''And a fusion engine?''

''Anachronistic,'' she said.

''Captain,'' said Kirsty Girard on the ship's communicator, ''it's all clear to board the alien.''

''Thank you, Kirsty,'' Josh said. ''Tell the ship's machinist to suit up and test my suit. We'll need two molecular disrupters.''

''Weapons?'' Girard asked,

''Side arms only.''

Pat Barkley, the ship's machinist, was waiting in the starboard air lock, bulky in E.V.A. gear. Angela helped Josh into his suit, closed the inner hatch, leaving the two men alone. Air hissed out of the lock and the outer hatch opened. Josh led the way out, spinning slightly when the awkward molecular disrupter caught on the side of the lock. The alien ship was just twenty feet away. Josh kicked over, moving very slowly, broke his movement with his right hand against the dark metal of the alien, said, ''Ouch, damnit,'' because, slow as he was moving, inertial force put a strain on his wrist, causing it to pop painfully. Pat Barkley landed lightly beside him, taking up the shock with his knees.

Josh secured his disrupter and released the umbilical that had attached him to the *Erin Kenner*. Barkley followed suit. Both men then secured themselves to the alien with a magnetic clamp attached to a line fed from the suit's belt and began to crawl over the hull of the small ship. She was the size of the *Erin Kenner*'s launch.

''Recognize the alloy?'' Josh asked Barkley.

''No, sir,'' Barkley said.

There were no visible seams. The ship's hull was as smooth as an egg, and as integrated. Josh ordered the *Erin Kenner* to move away to a safe distance.

"Okay, Pat," Josh said, picking up his cutting torch, "let's see what she's made of."

They worked side by side. The object was to cut out a square of metal from the ship's hull without damaging the tightly packed electronics inside. Josh fired off his disrupter, aimed the beam at the ship's metal, and saw it being reflected outward in a flaring flower.

"Whoa," Pat Barkley said. "What have we here?"

"You tell me," Josh said.

"Whatever it is, it's damned strong," Pat said. "And it would resist the heat at the surface of a star. Hold on, sir, and let me try another setting."

Pat adjusted his instrument, making the beam so fine that it could split atoms. The force no longer flared out. Slowly a small cut was being made in the odd metal. Pat gave the captain the setting. Josh began his own cut three feet away and parallel to Pat's.

"You're set a little deep, Captain," Pat said. "Cut the beam back two marks."

Josh obeyed. It took them almost an hour to remove a square of metal and expose the interior. Pat Barkley was examining the edges of the cut. "Captain, I think we'd better get Science to check out this metal. If I'm right, and if it's as heat resistant as I think it is, it might be very useful."

"In what way?"

Pat laughed. "Well, I'd guess in a lot of ways,

but I have a one-track mind and can think of only one at the moment. Back home I have an atmospheric racer. If I could put a skin of this stuff on its hull, I'd win every race there is. As you know, sir, there's almost no limit to how fast you can push a ship in atmosphere so far as sheer power is concerned. The limiting factor is the ablation factor of the metal in the ship's hull. In a good, tight race I burn off a full quarter-inch of metal. With this stuff—''

An image leapt into Josh's mind. A fiery object made a downward arc into atmosphere, flared to within two thousand feet of X&A headquarters, and went vertically back into space. A hull that could withstand speeds measured in thousands of feet per second in atmosphere would have made possible the wild, buzzing approach to headquarters, but why? You don't get out of a ship going so fast that it's nothing more than a glowing fireball.

''Secure samples, Pat, and we'll turn them over to Science.''

Beyond a thin layer of what looked like circuit boards there was a space of honeycomb construction. Each of the interstices was enclosed in a transparent material. Josh's initial efforts had not only sliced through the circuitry, but had opened one of the interstitial spaces. Liquid had condensed on the transparent surface. He inserted a test probe and the suit's tiny computer communicated information to the base unit aboard the *Erin Kenner* and reported almost instantly. Preliminary analysis indicated that the liquid was one of the amino acids.

Beyond the honeycomb was the solid metal side of the hydrogen fusion chamber. It wouldn't be healthy to cut into *that*.

"I think we've done about all we can without doing serious damage," Josh said.

"She's all engine, sir, with just a thin layer of electronics and the amino acid chambers under the outside hull."

"And the amino acid chambers are?"

Barkley shrugged inside his suit. "Computer storage chambers? Brain?"

"Primitive weaponry," Josh said. "Missiles that a city aircar could defeat. A rather stupid, head-on attack against a vastly superior ship. How do those things go with an alloy that could take a ship through sun flares and what seems to be an amino acid data storage system?"

They used shoulder jets to propel themselves back to the *Erin Kenner*. It was always a bit spooky to be flying free in space, and both men sighed in relief when they eased up to the ship's air lock and clamped on with magnetic spots.

Kirsty Girard was waiting for the captain on the bridge. "I've been running fine analysis on the metallic reading that lay closest to the surface," she said. "I want to show you two of them."

"Lead on," Josh said.

Kirsty activated a screen. First she showed Josh the overall view of an icy plain below a rise. "Here, the instruments detected metal quite close to the surface," she said. "I ran it through enhancement while you were E.V.A."

"And?" Josh asked.

"It's durametal, sir," Kirsty said. "Two durametal objects close enough together to show as one large metallic deposit on general scan."

"Two spaceships?" Josh asked, his heart pounding as he anticipated her answer.

"That's my guess, sir."

"Angela, have someone put a homing beacon on that ship out there so we can find it again when we want it," Josh ordered. "Kirsty, as soon as that's been done, take us down."

* * *

The *Erin Kenner* hovered two hundred feet above the elongated mound of ice and snow that hid two objects made of durametal. Josh, Angela, and Sheba were on the bridge, watching nervously as Kirsty tilted ship to play the exhaust of the flux drive over the mound. Water began to run down the slope of the mound only to refreeze quickly. It took two hours to expose the distinctive contours of a Zede luxury linor, another hour to melt away the ice that hid the name, *Fran Webster.*

All right, Kirsty," Josh said, his voice low. "Secure. Lift to orbit."

"But we haven't seen the other ship," Sheba protested. Her large emerald eyes were red with weeping.

"I don't think we have to, Queenie," Josh said. "I think you can bet that the other ship is the *Old Folks.*"

"They must have violated the first rule of exploration," Angela said.

"What's that?" Sheba asked.

"Even if you discover a place that looks,

smells, and states in large print that it's the Garden of Eden and there's a fellow there in a long white robe blessing you, don't land until Science has checked it out," Josh said.

From a stable orbit a robotic probe lowered itself on a tiny column of flux force. It landed near the *Fran Webster*. Already a white film was forming on the exposed metal of David Webster's Zede Starliner. The probe crawled past the luxury liner and began to play a heat beam over the mound of ice next to it. Optics aboard the probe soon showed an open hatch, and, on the ship's bow, the words *Old Folks*. Heat melted away ice that blocked the open hatch and soon the transmitter on the probe was beaming up a holoimage. Two humanoid forms lay side by side. Dan Webster had thrown his arm over Fran and that pose had been preserved in death.

"But I was told that they were alive," Sheba protested through tears.

The robot crawled back to the *Fran Webster*. The cutting properties of a molecular disrupter had to be used to gain entry. Sheba was still weeping silently, but when the hololens focused on the two humanoid forms encased in a sheen of ice she gasped and turned away. Both faces were recognizable. There was no doubt that the dead were David and Ruth Webster.

"Something's wrong," Sheba whispered.

"Yes, very wrong," Josh said bitterly. "They're dead."

"No, that's not what I mean," Sheba said, but she did not have to explain. Angela's face was

flushed. Josh averted his eyes. Only Sheba continued to stare in horror at the screen where her
brother and sister were frozen in an obscene coital
embrace.

CHAPTER TEN

Ordinarily a major vessel from the Department of Exploration and Alien Search would not have spent time and effort in the examination of an ice world. Most frozen planets were located far from the life-giving radiation of their star. The reference books were rich in examples ranging from the eighth and ninth planets of Sol, the sun of Old Earth, to hundreds of other lifeless orbs scattered throughout that relatively small zone of the galaxy which bounded the Confederation of the United Planets. After the reunion, when the mutated men of Old Earth became an integral part of the race, it was *de rigueur* for every institution of higher learning to end expeditions to Sol's solar system. No system in U.P. space had been more studied, and with the archaeological discovery of the original names of the nine planets there had developed a fad of applying the Old English names for the home planets as a generic label. Thus there were Mercurian planets and Saturnine planets and Plutonian planets.

Almost without exception all known planets could be classified by comparison with one of the nine pups of Old Sol. The planet which some of the crew of the *Erin Kenner* called Deep Freeze, the world that had killed four members of the Webster family, was that exception. She was encased in ice much like Pluto or the small moons of Uranus, but she was not at all like Pluto. Her core was molten, heavy metal, mostly iron. She had geological features which indicated that she had not always been buried beneath a blanket of snow and ice, which was interesting enough, but the feature of the planet that was most difficult to explain was illustrated by the blinding reflection of the sun from her white surface. She swam her orbit in a glare of light. So much solar energy fell on the surface that, according to Kirsty Girard's calculations, there should have been tropical jungles at her waist and great forests in her temperate areas, for the planet was definitely in the life zone of her sun.

The *Erin Kenner* kept a respectful distance above the surface. Before Captain Josh Webster allowed anyone to set foot on the planet, there were some things to be explained. The inept attack on the *Erin Kenner* by an unmanned ship was a physical manifestation of the overall mystery of the planet. The failure of two well-engineered and maintained spaceships and the deaths of four people aboard them was a sobering reminder that there were things unknown encased in the ice.

Both Josh and Sheba were achingly aware that their parents and siblings lay locked in the planet's frigid embrace. In the case of Ruth and David their shame was there for any observer to witness, and that bothered Josh almost as much as the basic question which was: Why the hell was the planet so cold when enough solar radiation poured down on her to melt all ice except, perhaps, for small areas near the poles?

The *Erin Kenner* was not equipped for efficient probings beneath the ice. In the normal course of events the X&A ship would have run a surface survey of the planet while conducting a thorough scan for life readings. Finding none in the ice, she would have recorded the ice planet's basic measurements, characteristics, and position in space in a claim of discovery for the people of the United Planets. Any utilization of the planet's resources would have been left to private sector prospectors and miners. A mining ship would be equipped with drill drones and probes that could, with relative ease, examine the metallic deposits under the ice.

Josh had three robotic exploration and test drones at his disposal, none of which was designed to burrow through ice. All three of the drones were at work. They measured a temperature well below zero at the surface of the ice while air temperatures a few feet above the ground indicated the strength of the sea of energy poured onto the planet by her sun. The drones began to pinpoint strong readings of metal beneath the ice and an interesting pattern emerged.

Kirsty Girard, in her role as science officer, called the captain into a small space packed with screens and dials and recording devices. "It gets a bit weird," she said, as she punched up a graphic on a monitor. "These large, pink areas are ore fields, some of them quite deep. They're pretty typical of a planet in the life zone."

"And those bright red spots?" Josh asked.

"I'm getting to that," Kirsty said. "That's the weird part." She punched buttons and the graphic expanded to take in a wider area. "So far the drones have covered most of the southern half of this large land mass. Take a look at the distribution of the red dots."

The dots formed a grid.

"The distance from dot to dot is uniform, almost exactly two hundred miles," Kirsty said. "As you can see by the color, each dot represents a highly concentrated mass of metal. Each one seems to be identical."

"Emanations? Electrical? Other?"

"None that we can detect," Kirsty said.

"How thick is the ice covering?"

"It varies, but there's at least two hundred feet of ice over the shallowest of the masses."

"Any doubt in your mind, Lieutenant Girard, that we've encountered the work of intelligent beings?"

A shiver went up and down Kirsty's spine. "None at all, sir."

"How long will it take to get the drones aboard?"

"Three hours."

"Okay. Start 'em up."

"Aye, sir," Kirsty said. "I wonder, sir, if I might have just a couple of hours?"

Josh waited.

"I've just started moving one of the drones." She pushed buttons and the image of the planet turned on the screen. A pointer stabbed toward an area of featureless white. "Here's another major land mass on the opposite side of the globe. I'd like to have a drone work there for a couple of hours to see if the same grid pattern of installations is in place."

Josh nodded. "I see no problem with that."

Sheba was with Angela on the control bridge. When Josh told them that they'd be blinking out toward the *Rimfire* route in about five hours, Angela sighed deeply. It had become apparent, with the attack of the unmanned drone, that the *Erin Kenner* had encountered an alien intelligence. She had not questioned Josh openly, but she'd felt then that it was time to back off and call in the headquarters boffins with their elaborate equipment and stringent safeguards.

Sheba said, "What about the bodies of our folks?"

"Queenie, they're a part of the whole. We couldn't touch them, even if I disobeyed regulations and common sense and sent a manned launch down to the surface."

"Josh, they'll see," Sheba said. "Everyone who comes here will see what Ruth and David were doing."

Josh shook his head regretfully. "Can't be helped, Queenie."

"My father and mother are down there," Sheba said with emotion. "He was born on Tigian II, and he loved it. You were sent a copy of his will. If you read it, you might remember that he provided that his and Mother's ashes be placed in the family memorial at T-Town. That meant a lot to him, because that memorial holds the ashes of six generations of Websters. He provided a place for each of us, too, Josh. There are niches for Ruth and David.''

''We can request that the remains be sent there when X&A has completed its investigation,'' Josh said.

''Josh, damnit, I don't know what kind of a place this is, or what the hell went on down there, but I know damned well that what Ruth and David were doing when they died was not their idea.''

''No, I guess not,'' Josh said.

''You could separate them with one of the drones,'' Sheba said.

''Queenie, if a drone touches them, they'll shatter. We haven't been able to get exact temperature readings of frozen objects such as a bone, or the metal of the ships. We know that objects alien to this planet are much colder than the very thin air around them. Kirsty Girard thinks that it's close to absolute zero in the interior of the metals that shattered on touch, and that would hold true for the bodies. At that temperature durasteel crumbles like a cracker. Try to separate David and Ruth and we'd have a pile of frozen chips of flesh and bone.''

''Which could be decently cremated,'' Sheba said.

''No,'' Josh said. ''I'm sorry.''

''Captain,'' said Kirsty Girard's voice on the communicator, ''can you come to Science and Navigation?''

''On my way, Kirsty,'' Josh said.

Both Angela and Sheba followed him to stand in the door to Kirsty's ''office'' as Josh leaned over a monitor. They could both see a darkness in a field of white ice.

As Josh watched, the dark spot resolved itself into a square cube of metal. The drone was airborne, and was closing on the structure.

"Why didn't we spot this before?" Josh asked.

"Because up until about one hour ago it was covered by two hundred feet of ice," Kirsty said. "I had the area on camera, a wide view, when the ice began to melt. The computer alerted me to the change in image. It took only sixteen minutes for the ice cover to be removed."

Josh felt a prickle of alarm at the nape of his neck. She had phrased her words to indicate that she believed that the dull metal square had been deliberately revealed by someone or by something.

"Keep the drone at two miles distance," Josh ordered. "Readout?"

Kirsty was controlling the drone with eye and head movements inside a snug-fitting helmet. She hovered the drone and ordered use of all of its sensors.

"No emissions. No radiation. No heat," she said.

"Bring the drone home," Josh said.

"Wait," Kirsty said, with excitement in her voice. "The shell of that square is made of the same metal that was in the hull of the ship that attacked us. No wonder we're getting no readings. That stuff would keep heat or any emissions inside."

"Bring it home, Kirsty," Josh ordered calmly.

"Yes, sir," Kirsty said. She thought the order.

The drone moved swiftly, darting directly toward the metal cube protruding above the ice.

"Watch it," Josh said.

"Come back, damn you," Kirsty grated between her teeth as the drone settled onto the smooth top of the cube. She looked up at Josh, her eyes wide. "It's all right," she said. "There's no danger."

Josh felt a sense of relief. A great peace settled over him. "No," he said, "there is no danger."

"We can get Ruth and David now," Sheba said.

For a moment Angela felt protest rising in her, but she, too, felt the great sense of peace and rightness. She smiled.

"Kirsty, send a drone down to the *Fran Webster.* Use the earth sampler scoop to gather up the two bodies. Seal them in a specimen bag."

"They'll be mixed together," Sheba said.

"They died together," Angela said.

"We can try to gather them in separately," Josh said.

Angela felt protest rising again, sensed that something was very wrong, tried to overcome the powerful sense of well-being that engulfed her. She moved toward the drone control panel, forcing each step. Her limbs were heavy. Her feet seemed to be anchored in thick, heavy mud. She lifted a control helmet.

"Better let Kirsty do it, Angel," Josh said. "She's more accustomed to the peculiarities of each drone."

"Yes, all right," Angela said.

Kirsty had switched away from the drone that rested atop the dark cube of metal on the other side of the world. She was directing one of the returning drones to reverse direction and go down to the surface again.

"I'll just monitor," Angela said, and her movements became more free. She put out her hand and touched a switch and felt the control contact with the drone atop the cube. She braced herself and gave the order. The drone shifted position and on the screen a bright speck of fire appeared as it extended the nozzle of a molecular cutting torch and began to slice into the metal of the cube.

"Angela, what the hell—" Josh began. The rest of his question was cut off by a flare of light on the screen as the drone disintegrated.

Angela made one small sound as she toppled to the deck. Josh bent over her, removed the helmet. He cried out harshly, a painful, strained male scream. The beautiful emerald eyes had been exploded out of their sockets. Blood ran from her ears and her nose, and her skull, as he extended his hand and touched her, was soft. He withdrew his hand quickly and looked at his fingers. They were covered with blood and something else, a white paste. It was as if her brain had exploded inside her skull, shattering and pulping the bone, oozing out into her long, blonde hair.

Before either Kirsty or Sheba could react, Josh was at the console. He punched in a quick order, took weapons control, and within seconds a laser beam lanced downward, curved around the horizon. Kirsty, guessing what Josh intended, focused another viewer on the cube of metal on the far continent. She gasped as she saw that it was already almost hidden by ice.

The laser beam exploded on target. It was some time before the viewers could see through the resulting cloud of steam and fragments. When the view was clear, there was a large crater where the cube had been, and even as Josh and the others watched the ice began to melt and cover the crater with a swiftly forming lake of clear water.

Josh was searching out the next target. Once again the beam lanced down and there was another crater and an expanding area of melt as another cube was destroyed.

Kirsty put her arms around Josh and tried to pull his hands away from the console. "Captain," she said, "that's enough."

"They killed her," Josh said, his voice full of agony. "The bastards killed her."

"Captain, please," Kirsty begged, as another cube and the mass of ice surrounding it was vaporized. "You can't do this. You've got to stop it."

With great effort, Josh controlled his rage. He fell to his knees beside Angela. There was a great deal of blood on the deck.

CHAPTER ELEVEN

When the Watcher was alerted for the second time, the planet had made less than one orbit around its sun since the last trespass. A check of systems, the first priority from the day of the beginning, showed need for nourishment in distant ganglia. A healing flow of electrons swept outward to bring all extensions to full readiness within seconds.

The second intrusion was at the site of the first. Such exact positioning could not be accidental. The Watcher waited. Unlike the first one, the second intruder made no immediate attempt at penetration or exploration. There was time for a thorough study of the aliens and their craft. It only took a moment to determine that the occupants of the ship were the same as the first pair. The spaceship was more interesting. The propulsion system was of the same unknown type as that of the smaller ship. The drive, itself, was of simple construction, but it had taken a full concentration of reasoning power to determine that the plant utilized magnetic-radiative power, the energy of the stars. The small ship had been impressive. This second, large ship was even more advanced and required much study. A stream of observations flowed along lengthy ganglia and was stored.

The life-support systems of the two ships told the Watcher much about the psysiology of the two life-forms even before a careful probe of thought patterns was initiated. The forces of creation had allowed prodigious latitude in the variety of life-forms but the basic mechanics of intelligent life were that the development of intelligence had not been confined to one planet more blessed than others, as it had once been believed. But then, the very existence of the Watcher and the necessity for eternal vigilance was conclusive testimony to the doctrine of parallel creation.

The intruders, like the first two, breathed oxygen and were carbon based. They were bipedal. In short, they were alien only by definition, not in construction or appearance.

The Watcher waited. Certain aspects of their science were disturbing. The apparently easy discovery of the smaller ship by the newcomers raised questions. Tendrils of energy penetrated the ship's hull and began to search out a pathway through a more formidable barrier, the natural defense of the aliens' consciousness.

The first ship had been equipped with sophisticated subsurface exploration machinery. It was a mining vessel in search of ores. The function of the second ship was not so easily determined. It had complex communication equipment and carried weapons which, if properly applied, could do damage to sensory ganglia near the surface.

The question that most needed answering was how the large vessel so easily located the smaller one. The planet's ice hid more than one secret. During the first few years of the Watcher's vigil more than one ship had strayed onto the ice, and a few had come deliberately. They had, of course, been silenced, and their repose had gone undisturbed, along with that of the Sleepers, across the millennia while the planet swam its path around the sun and the disc of the galaxy rotated ponderously. As the centuries slipped past, nothing puzzled the Watcher beyond a simple demand for silencing—and not even that for thousands of years—until the second intruder landed next to the icy tomb of the early trespassers.

How did the second alien ship locate the first so quickly and so precisely? The silencing of the first intruders had been quick and effective. No call had gone out into space from the meddler's voice communications system.

It was possible that the larger ship contained metal detection equipment more effective than any known to the Watcher. The relatively tiny amount of metal in the first ship could not be easily sorted out from the mass of ore that lay under her, at least not by any method known to the Watcher. The Watcher consulted a vast store of information and confirmed the first belief that the smaller ship could not have communicated its whereabouts.

The answers lay within the minds of the interlopers. The Watcher pushed and probed with invisible tendrils to find that the defensive shell of the female's mind was stronger and more difficult to deceive than that of the male. Penetration came when the male realized that the frozen mass at his feet was the bodies of his parents. In that moment of great emotion the alien mind lost tension. The Watcher noted the entity's feeling of loss and fear as nothing more than pure data.

The alien's defenses were back in place quickly. Entry could be forced, but not without massive damage. The use of force would preclude any opportunity to gain the information needed to answer the Watcher's questions. The Watcher waited, probing softly, soothingly. The emotion that the aliens identified as sorrow gave the Watcher entry into the female's mind. Tendrils of energy tested and cataloged, but the needed answers were still hidden.

The Watcher's pure intellect was not clouded by the enigmatic brew of hormonal and glandular secretions. The Watcher's thoughts sped along indestructible circuits and did not have to depend on the electrochemical interchanges through biological material. The Watcher searched for a point of weakness and found it in the female's emotions. Soon tendrils found the same small chink in the male's defenses. The Watcher did not have to understand emotion to utilize it. The Watcher did not feel superior. It is a wise intellect that knows its limitations and its origins. However, it was good that the Watcher was not weakened by the distractions of emotion, and even more fortunate that the reproduction mechanism of the aliens was quite similar to that of the Sleepers and, therefore, familiar. It was through that pathway that the Watcher moved. It was a simple matter to chart the workings of the reproduction system and to stimulate certain areas of the brain.

The Watcher moved into the libido of the female's mind and dictated an arousal. Next, the ebullient passions of the male were the Watcher's target, and so intense was the stimulation that the desired results were achieved and the two aliens were locked together with the flow of hormonal juices dominating both mind and body. The Watcher penetrated. The functions of the small black box in the heart of the ship's reason center were noted, thus answering the most important question. This piece of technology was new to the Watcher, but the Watcher did not know the feeling of surprise. There was only acceptance. In the future silencing would have to be performed more quickly with specific attention being given to the black box.

The same device was in place on the second vessel, but now the Watcher knew and could check the broadcast bands utilized by the emergency device. No signal was being sent, but that did not mean that one had not been sent before the Watcher scanned the spectrum. It was necessary to take steps to assure that a future trespasser would not be able to locate the two ships through a signal from the black box. The Watcher sent silence into the ship's reason center and searched out the black box. Within seconds all molecular motion in and around the instrument was slowed. For millennia that method of silencing had been sufficient, but now the Watcher went further. The force of silence was intensified. The black box crumbled into dust.

Even while taking quick and positive action to prevent a signal being sent from the ship, the Watcher had been seeking. The coming of the second ship had not been accidental. There was a family tie between the two sets of aliens. The first two had come seeking metals. The second two had come because of the family ties. There were other members of the family. The family tie had brought a second ship, therefore it would bring a third. An additional danger was represented by the signal sent by the black box of the first ship. The Watcher searched. The transmission that had been picked up by the larger ship was still traveling outward through space, but with each passing moment it was becoming more diffuse and it was less likely that it would be detected by another ship in the vastness of the galaxy. That threat diminished, there remained the probability that other members of the family would come looking.

The Watcher decided on immediate action. Orders traveled swiftly along sensitive ganglia. On a mountainside, where the ice cover was relatively thin, melting occurred. Long dormant circuits were activated. A hum of power came from the fusion engine of an extension. A door rolled away and the extension soared, hovered, and flashed out of existence to travel the long route traced by both of the aliens' ships. Those ships, the first to disturb the sleep of the ice planet in millennia, had come a long way, not only in space but in time. The mission of the extension was twofold.

The minds of the aliens, drugged by hormone stimulated electrochemical activity in the synapses of the brain, were open for the taking. The Watcher knew all.

The silencing was not designed or intended to be merciful, for that concept was unknown to the

Watcher. Silencing was simply quick. In the throes of mindless, artificially stimulated passion the male and female stiffened as one. Cold lanced through soft flesh. The flow of blood ceased. Liquids solidified. Cells burst. The aliens died so quickly that their last thoughts were storms of erotic fulfillment.

CHAPTER TWELVE

The space arm of the Department of Exploration and Alien Search traced many of its traditions back to Terra II, the planet that was also called New Earth. There the stranded travelers from Old Earth, having lost all stored data in the crash landing of their primitive ship, had begun the long, arduous climb back into space. With only the knowledge held in the frail chalice of memory, their task was to rebuild the technological culture that had sent man into the near space of Old Earth on bellowing pillars of explosive fire. They had the good seeds of Old Earth, wheat and corn and other grains, root vegetables and leaf vegetables, fruits, nuts, and berries; and they had the living embryos of the familiar and useful animals of their world, sheep, cattle, and horses. Where man went there was the animal that he had first domesticated, the dog. And with his old friend beside him man began the long journey back.

According to those who held the belief put forward by the one piece of Old Earth knowledge that survived the first and only Terran settlement among the stars, the Bible, God had chosen the rich, friendly planet that was to be called New Earth. The soils were fertile, the land masses extensive. There were mountains and oceans and native flora that was not hostile to the transplanted animals and Earth vegetation. The raw materials were there for the eventual rise of industry and technology.

The way back was not to be traveled swiftly, although the result of the crash of the starship was not a return to savagery. Crude metal tools were made from the broken shell of the ship and from the intact laboratory came draft animals to pull wooden plows. So the culture fell not to barbarism but to the level of subsistence farming. Many of those who survived knew the theory of refining iron from ore, but the ship's metallurgist, and most of the other scientific specialists, had been killed in the crash. The technical library had disappeared forever, along with the rest of the electronically stored knowledge of mankind, with the destruction of the ship's computer system.

Everyone knew that there was such a thing as an electric light bulb, but the technology needed to make it possible to push a switch and say, "Let there be light" had to begin with something as basic as making a wheel. When you have only crude tools, and you haven't the means or the skills to work metals, you can make wooden wheels and mount them on wooden axles and build a frame atop them and you have a wagon, but that's just one tiny step toward the generation of electricity.

As the centuries came and went, progress was faster than it had been in the rise of mankind on

Old Earth, because it was known that it was possible to push a switch and flood a room with light, because the knowledge of what once was—although dimmed by time and dilution—was both a goal and a goad. The relatively small group of space travelers had obeyed the biblical injunction to go forth and multiply. Explorers mapped a continent. Ships sailed the oceans and spread man to the other land masses. With the growth of technical knowledge the resources of the planet were utilized. Steam engines replaced sails on the seas and the internal combustion engine was not far behind.

And then man was back in the sky, reaching with accelerated eagerness toward space. Somewhere out there, its exact location long since forgotten, was Home. Earth. The Mother Planet. The myth. All knowledge of the original planet had been passed down by word of mouth in the beginning, and the telling had been colored by the fears and bitterness of the original exiles. Old Earth was a place of savagery. It was a world of war and death. Diverse peoples who spoke languages understood only by themselves sought to dominate others, to take spoils and exact tribute. Old Earth was a planet of carnivores. Man, himself, was the most dangerous of all. The cities of Old Earth were walled and men had to be ready at all times to defend what was theirs. It was to escape the cycle of wars and destruction that the original settlers had set forth into the unknown. To prevent the reinstitution of war as policy, the old ones taught peace, but they remembered. Although there was no threat to man on New Earth from members of his own race or from carnivorous animals, the first settlement had a thorn barricade. On Old Earth a nation had to be capable of defending itself or fall prey to the first aggressor who came along. This basic philosophy was so much a part of man that as technology developed and population grew New Earth organized an army and a navy.

In defense of having armed forces on a planet populated by one unified people those who were elected to govern pointed upward, toward the darkness of space. "We came through the distances," they said. "Others might, as well."

The most common explanation for the army and the navy was that it gave the young ones something to do during two to four critical years in their development. When, as they had on Old Earth, the thundering rockets began to maul their way out of the atmosphere, a new service was organized. The space arm became *The* Service. Members of The Service tested the first ship to be equipped with a blink generator. Man had managed, once again, to reach out to the stars.

Later, when a small explorer ship happened into the sac in which swam the Dead Worlds, xenophobia was given new impetus. The people who had destroyed an entire family of worlds, actually cooling the interior fires of planets, were out there somewhere. Those fearsome beings with weapons which man could only imagine could come sweeping out of the depths of space at any time. X&A ships went armed, and because of the Dead Worlds there was developed a weapon as awesome as that which the killer race had used to cool the fires of the Dead Worlds, the planet buster. One missile, one planet. One titanic convulsion and there was a new asteroid belt where once there had been a world.

To man's eternal shame, the planet buster was used in the Zede War, a conflict that pitted man against man once more. The Zede worlds boasted the finest technology in the galaxy, and, although they were outnumbered by those loyal to the United Planets Confederation, they were close to victory when "in the interest of freedom and the dignity of mankind" the United Planets began to fire the deadly, planet destroying missiles.

So it was that the Service had its roots in the history of what the mutants of Old Earth called The Old Ones, the original race of man as represented by those few who managed to escape Earth before The Destruction. When a sailing ship of the New Earth Navy lost a man while at sea, his body was consigned to the deep with due cer emony. Traveling in the broad cavity of space was, in many ways, similar to sailing wide seas. In each instance distance was a factor, and time was required to conquer that distance. When a man died far from land on one of the old sailing ships, he was sewn into a hank of sail and given to the sea. There the materials contained in his body were returned to the earth through decay. In deep space a ship was far from home. Aboard a relatively small vessel, such as the *Erin Kenner,* no method had been provided for storing a dead body. Even on larger ships keeping a body aboard would have been entirely too destructive of crew morale. Better to consign the dead to the sea, to the sea of space.

However, there was a difference between dumping a man's body into the water where it would be consumed by sea creatures who would benefit from it and pushing a body through an air lock to float in the darkness of space. There the cold and the vacuum would preserve the body forever. Although the cosmos could have accepted the fleshy remains of all mankind without becoming noticeably littered, it had become the custom, early on, to give the dead a gentle thrust toward the nearest sun. Perhaps the idea of one's remains floating weightlessly through eternity in the loneliness of the big black had contributed to the adoption of the custom. Perhaps it was just a reflection of the accepted way of disposing of the dead through cremation. Or, perhaps there was a smidgen of comfort for the survivors in knowing that their comrade would not be cold forever.

Angela Bardeen Webster, forty-five years old, not yet halfway through her allotted lifespan, was consigned to space in a Service bodybag. The *Erin Kenner* was driving on flux toward the sun that reflected off the ice of the second planet of the system. Joshua Webster, in E.V.A. gear, stood in the lock beside his wife's body as the air was evacuated and the outer lock opened to the void. He knelt beside the bundle and put his gloved hand on it. He said a prayer with much hesitation, for he was not ordinarily a praying man. He took the bodybag in his arms. He leaned against his safety line and, after a long pause, pushed the bodybag away. The speed at which both the ship and the body were moving was not apparent. The body tumbled, moving slowly away from the ship, and, at the same time, continued along the vector imparted by the *Erin Kenner*'s motion. Weeks later, a tiny mote in the glare of solar fires, it would be consumed, its components returned to the cosmos.

Josh watched the tumbling bundle until it was lost in the distance. He felt the clang of metal on metal as the outer hatch closed, heard air roar into the lock. Sheba and Kirsty Girard were in the service corridor waiting for him. Sheba helped him get out of his suit, took his hand, kissed him on the cheek. He pushed her gently away.

"Lieutenant Girard."

"Aye, sir."

"Take us back to DF-2."

The crew had taken to calling the ice planet Deep Freeze and that name had been applied to the entire system. Thus the second planet from the sun was Deep Freeze II, DF-2.

"Sir?"

"I think I spoke quite clearly," Josh said.

"Aye, sir," Kirsty said.

The navigator hurried ahead of them. Josh and Sheba walked more slowly, arriving on the control bridge in time to feel the slide of a blink as Kirsty moved ship. DF-2 gleamed whitely on the viewers. Kirsty had blinked the ship directly into the orbit she had last occupied. Directly below them lay the two Webster ships.

"We're going to get them," Josh said to Sheba. "We're going to take our family home."

At the controls, Kirsty looked startled. She licked her lips nervously.

"Are you sure that's the right thing to do, Josh?" Sheba asked.

"It's what I'm going to do," he said. "That bastard down there has taken enough from me." He thumbed on the ship's communicator. "This is the captain speaking," he said. "As you know an act of aggression has been committed against this ship. We do not intend to accept this outrage without retaliation. The installation that directed the attack which resulted in the death of one of this ship's crew had been destroyed. Soon we will be returning to the out-galaxy blink route where we can make contact with headquarters to ask for a complete alien contact team. In the meantime we have a duty to perform. Down there on that planet lie the bodies of four of our people. As you may have heard, they are all my relatives. That is not the prime consideration. The important thing is that we have always given our dead a proper burial and that's what I intend to do with those down there on the surface."

Kirsty looked at Sheba and raised her eyebrows in surprise.

"Because of the condition of the bodies, recovery will be a delicate operation," Josh continued. "It cannot be accomplished by remote."

"Whooo," Kirsty whispered.

"I will lead the landing party," Josh said. "I'll need three volunteers."

"Pat Barkley, Captain," a voice said immediately. "I'll go."

In quick succession the rest of the crew repeated Pat's offer.

"Thank you," Josh said. "I'm going to designate Pat Barkley as my second on the surface. Pat, I'll leave it to you to pick the other two men."

When Josh turned off the communicator, Kirsty cleared her throat.

"Yes, Lieutenant Girard?" Josh asked.

"May I speak frankly, sir?"

"If you'll make it fast."

"If you land, you'll be breaking so many service regulations that it will take an hour of computer time just to list them," Kirsty said.

"But there is one regulation, Lieutenant, that supercedes all of the others," Josh said. "In space the captain's best judgment is the final criterion."

"Yes, sir," Kirsty said.

"You'll be senior aboard ship while I'm E.V.A.," Josh said. "I want Weapons on the alert. I want you to be ready to blast anything that moves, and if there's any real problem down there you are hereby ordered to use maximum force, if necessary, to insure the safety of this ship and her crew."

"Aye, sir," Kirsty said. She swallowed with difficulty, for her throat closed up as she absorbed the meaning of the captain's order. Maximum force, aboard an X&A ship, meant use of the galaxy's most terrible weapon, the planet buster.

The landing party was away within minutes. Kirsty felt the reaction of the *Erin Kenner* to the separation of the ship's launch. She adjusted a viewer and had the little vessel on screen as it fell away toward the gleaming surface.

"You're against this, aren't you?" Sheba asked.

"Very much so," Kirsty said. "Has your brother always been impulsive?"

"Anything but," Sheba said.

"Kirsty," Josh's voice said from the communicator, "we're at fifty thousand feet. We'll be landing in about ten minutes. All systems on the alert?"

"We're ready, Captain," Erin said.

"Good. Stand by."

"Standing by," Kirsty said.

The ship was in a stationary orbit directly over the landing site. DF-2's thin, clear atmosphere made for excellent visibility of the surface. Together Kirsty and Sheba watched the launch settle down toward the ice. Kirsty was finding it difficult to believe that an X&A captain was disobeying, along with others, the two prime commandments regarding exploration and alien contact. Not only was the captain landing on a planet that had not been declared safe by the science division of the service, he had, in effect, declared war on an alien intelligence without so much as having sent available data back to headquarters.

She was thinking that she was setting herself up for a reprimand at best and a court martial at worst when she ordered the preparation of a standard permanent blink beacon. When the beacon was ready she activated its memory banks and, in one huge, electronic gulp, copied the entire contents of the *Erin Kenner*'s computer into them.

"Hold on to your stomach," she told Sheba.

"Kirsty," said the voice of Josh Webster, "we're five minutes from touchdown."

"Standing by," Kirsty said, even as she pushed the button that would send the *Erin Kenner* six light-years into space. It took exactly two minutes and five seconds to kill the ship's movement relative to the stars and to plant the blink beacon. Two minutes and ten seconds after she had blinked away from DF-2, the ship was back in position.

"How's it going, Captain?" she sent.

"All quiet below," Josh said. "Two minutes away from touchdown."

"Keep talking, Captain," Kirsty said.

"One minute thirty and counting."

Apparently Josh was not aware that the ship had been light-years away from the ice planet. Kirsty would inform him, of course, but not at such a critical time. She didn't see how he could object to her having taken out a small insurance policy by planting a blink beacon out toward the periphery and the *Rimfire* route, a beacon that would be checked by any ship that passed nearby. Of course, no ship would find the beacon unless it was following the course of the two dead vessels below and the *Erin Kenner*. But if, God forbid, things were to go very, very wrong for the captain and his landing party, and if that wrongness somehow affected the *Erin Kenner*, at least there'd be a record of events prior to the captain's landing on the surface. If the unthinkable happened and the *Erin Kenner* joined the two civilian ships on Deep Freeze, whoever came next to DF-2 would reach the planet with the knowledge that a deadly threat lay beneath the ice.

CHAPTER THIRTEEN

At first the Watcher considered the silencing of the female aboard the orbiting ship to be a mistake. The swift and deadly reaction of the intruder had caused serious damage to the network. Repair facilities were inadequate to counter total destruction. However, the trespasser had localized his attack in an area where the consequent thinning of the concealing cover of ice would reveal nothing more than a rocky plateau. In time, power could be increased in neighboring installations to extend the ice thinly over the affected area.

A hum of activity surged around the globe as a system of rerouted impulses isolated the mangled ganglia in the damaged units. When disrupted communications had been reestablished with all modules the Watcher reconsidered and determined that having seized the opportunity to strike within the enemy's ship, rather than having been ill-advised, had been the catalyst needed to gain a measure of control over the situation.

The raging emotions rising from the death of his mate gave the Watcher total access to the male who was the leader of the latest group of intruders. Influencing the others aboard the ship was proving to be more difficult. The inability to take command immediately, as had always been possible from the beginning, caused the Watcher to work to full capacity seeking an explanation. There were two interesting possibilities. Although the Watcher was self-renewing and thus for all practical purposes immortal, there was, as had been predicted by the Designers, a small amount of erosion of efficiency due to age. That was one feasible explanation for failure to command the intruders until they were distracted by strong emotions. It was possible, too, that the Designers had not properly anticipated the results of passing ages on the process of creation and evolution.

This last prospect was not to be seriously considered, for the Watcher's reasoning ability was based not only on the knowledge of the Designers but reflected their attitudes and prejudices. The Designers had known that the Sleepers would not be left to their dreamless rest for eternity. It was in the nature of things that someone would come. Somewhere among the stars the processes that had produced the Sleepers had been, were and would forever be in action and it was inevitable that beings of intelligence would be curious about the ice-shrouded planets, for life zone planets were the prized jewels of the galaxy, and as rare.

They had come and while it was true that certain aspects of their technology were impressive, it was still as the Designers had predicted. The newcomers were not the equal of that which had been. In fact, the inferiority of Man was easily illustrated by his lack of understanding of the silencing cold, and by his unawareness of the Watcher's intrusion into his mind.

However, several aspects of the confrontation with the beings who called themselves Man generated accelerated activity in the Watcher's reason center. The purpose was clear, to silence, to protect the Sleepers. It had seemed simple at first and the ease with which the first two intruders had been silenced had lulled the Watcher into complacency. When the second ship landed, the web of complications had become apparent and logic had dictated—since family ties had instigated its coming—that others of the same family would follow. It had been deemed necessary to silence brothers and sisters of the two who had come seeking their parents, and as quickly as possible. Extensions had been sent to the alien worlds to expedite that desired end by implanting in the minds of the other members of the family the compulsion to find their missing relatives.

That the brother, Joshua Webster, was a representative of government was an unfortunate coincidence, and that was one of the Watcher's concerns. The likelihood of further complications became more probable when the female left in charge of the enemy ship placed a communications device in space where the next searcher would be sure to find it. The Watcher had tried and failed to prevent that action, but even as Joshua Webster approached the two dead ships on the planet's surface, measures were being taken to prevent the distribution of the information contained in the device. From the south polar region an extension lifted into space, shielding itself from the enemy's detection instruments by keeping the mass of the planet between itself and the alien ship's sensors. And at installations situated in a circle around the two frozen vessels on the surface instruments that had not been used since the beginning were activated and held ready for animation.

* * *

Josh was the first to step out of the launch onto the ice. Pat Barkley followed him. Pat and the two crewmen who completed the landing party were armed with heavy duty saffer rifles. Josh felt heavy and clumsy, for he had ordered that thermal shells be worn over the E.V.A. gear. The addition of the space armor added fifty pounds to the weight of the gear. The shell's special alloys would have allowed a man to work safely on the sun side of the first planet, where the storm of the solar wind flared down with lethal force. Scientists had used the thermal shell to walk within spitting distance of the lava flow of an active volcano. The shell would deflect a direct blast from a small laser weapon and would be intact, although the man inside might be dead from concussion, after a direct hit from a saffer.

Josh was taking no chances. He led the way to the *Old Folks*. Barkley and the two crewmen maneuvered two specimen recovery vehicles toward the ships, left one of them at the bow of the *Fran Webster*. The other, its small flux engine purring, floated under guidance into the open lock of the *Old Folks*.

For long moments Josh stood looking down at the frozen remains of his parents. He had seen them on the ship's viewers and it had not seemed real. His reason had told him they were dead, but it was not until he stood over them, saw through the coating of ice the terrible damage that had been done to flesh by rupturing cells, that the total impact of their death hit him.

"Shall I begin, Captain?" Pat Barkley asked.

For a moment he was tempted to say no, to leave them as they were with his father's arm around his mother's waist. Yes."

Barkley used a small molecular disrupter to cut the frozen bodies free from the ice that bound them to the deck of the ship. Finished, he secured the torch and stood back as the crewmen positioned the specimen recovery bin near the bodies. Working space was limited in the control room of the tug, and completion of the task was slowed by the awkwardness and bulk of the thermal shells. It took all four of them to lift the two frozen bodies and the ice that still encased them. The two crewmen let their burden slip from their hands before it touched the bottom of the bin and ice shattered. Josh sucked in his breath, for he feared that the impact would cause the frozen flesh of his parents to shard and splinter like the ice.

"Okay, fine," Pat Barkley said, as he closed the recovery bin. "Let's get the hell out of here."

A crewman guided the bin toward the open hatch.

"Imagination is a powerful thing," Pat Barkley said as he stepped out of the ship. "I can almost feel the cold."

Josh shivered. He, too, had been thinking that it was his imagination. The thermal shell protected against cold as well as heat.

* * *

The Watcher waited until the four men were inside the smaller of the two ships. They were in contact with the surface through the ice-encased hull. The Watcher flowed the energy of the silencing into the metal of the ship. Nothing happened. The answer was found in the mind of Joshua Webster. The Watcher recorded the data regarding the thermal shell and ordered still another total review of all information. The density of the silencing cold was amplified. For hundreds of miles around the site silencer modules were brought to full power.

As the four men moved heavily toward the larger ship, taking with them the bodies of the first two intruders, the Watcher ordered animation of the newly activated mobile extensions. The cold, the weapon that had never failed, was ineffective against the thermal shield. The action that was ordered was risky. Timing had to be exact. It would take time to reach the orbiting ship. The men on the ground must be prevented from giving alarm. The Watcher was certain in his logic center that Man's claim to be able to reduce a planet to rubble was vainglorious boasting, but there was certain knowledge that the warship above had weapons that could cause bothersome damage.

The first of the mobile extensions was lifted to the surface from an underground chamber. It was the color of the ice. It moved quickly and smoothly toward the invaders. It had been fashioned in the image of the Designers, but was more sure-footed as it leapt from hummock to hummock, ran smoothly across a flat plain, and approached the downed ships from the blind side.

Meanwhile, mobile extensions as black as the face of space lifted off under their own internal power to angle upward toward the orbit of the alien ship.

The Watcher saw all, recorded all, and while functioning on several different levels probed into the mind of the man to whom access had been attained. The emotions which were known to the man as anger and sadness were still in dominance. It was a simple matter to keep the man to his purpose. The group of four entered the larger of the two ships, the empty specimen collector floating along easily in front of one of the crewmen.

* * *

"So far so good," Josh radioed to the *Erin Kenner*. "We have the bodies from *Old Folks*. We're going into the *Fran Webster* for the others." He avoided calling the dead by name. That would have been too painful. He led the way. When he saw David and Ruth frozen in sexual union, his throat was so dry that he could not swallow.

Pat was feeling the cold. His lips were numb. He looked at the frozen mass, the female legs locked around the back of the man, all of it made more than obscene by the damage done when freezing cells expanded and ruptured.

"Cap'n, what in hell are we up against?" Pat asked.

Josh shook his head.

"Kirsty Girard swept this ice ball from pole to pole looking for life signals," Pat said. "She didn't find any."

"Well, it will be up to the big brains from headquarters to figure it out," Josh said. "Let's do it."

Once again the cutting beam of a molecular disrupter was used to separate the frozen bodies from the deck. Once again four men strained and slipped and grunted to put the mass in the specimen bin.

"Erin Kenner," Josh sent, "this is the captain. Mission accomplished. We're coming up."

"Acknowledged, Captain," said Kirsty Girard from the *Erin Kenner.*

The crewmen started the bin toward the hatch. Josh looked around and felt his anger surge again. The *Fran Webster* had been a beautiful ship. His brother had worked hard for decades to be able to own such a masterpiece of the shipbuilders' craft and it had been taken from him without apparent reason. At the moment that seemed almost as offensive as David's death. Four members of the Webster family had come to DF-2 without warlike aims and they were dead. He took one last look around. The beautifully constructed instrument panel of the Zede Starliner was distorted by a layer of clear ice. The ship was dead. Even the residual power in the blink generator had been drained away, and that was damned odd. As long as a generator was within view of a star it collected and held power.

Suddenly the image of a star cluster with sterile orbiting planets flashed into his mind and he looked over his shoulder quickly as he felt a flush of disease. Killing a blink generator down to cold stop was not nearly as difficult as cooling the molten core of a world, but the images were similar.

He saw that the crewmen were almost at the hatch. Pat was directly behind them. He shrugged his shoulders under the load of the thermal shield and took one step.

One of the crewmen cried out in surprise as the hatch was filled with whiteness that resolved itself into humanoid shape.

"Captain?" said the other crewman as the white figure moved.

"Watch it," Pat Barkley yelled, trying to bring the muzzle of his saffer to bear on the thing in the hatch.

"Fire," Josh ordered, lifting his own rifle only to find the body of one of the crewmen between him and the hatch.

The explosion was contained within the hull of the *Fran Webster.* A shock wave rushed past the white figure in the hatch without displacing it. It leapt forward and pushed the floating specimen bin out of the way. The four men had been tossed about by the explosion. Quickly the extension opened the visors of the thermal shells and with its fist smashed the helmets of the E.V.A.s.

Josh Webster was conscious when he looked up into the icy face, saw a pair of glowing eyes, saw dexterous fingers moving toward the visor of his shell.

"Kirsty," he whispered, as he nudged open the communicator with his chin.

"Yes, Captain."

"Kirsty—" He could not form the words he was bellowing in his mind. He was thinking, "Shoot, shoot, shoot. Blast him, Kirsty. Max force."

He said, "Kirsty, we're coming up."

"That's an affirmative," Kirsty said. "We have the launch on viewer."

The cold ended Josh's agony of self-blame.

* * *

"Bridge, Weapons."

"Go, Weapons."

"Kirsty, I'm getting ghost images on short-range detection."

"Show me," Kirsty said.

A viewer came to life. Against a black background a glowing image moved.

"Mass about two hundred pounds," Weapons said. "Size roughly three by six feet. And the sonofabitch is invisible, it seems."

"What shows it?"

"Infrared only."

"Shoot it," Kirsty said.

"Shoot it?"

"Now," Kirsty ordered.

A lance of fire went out from the bow of the ship. There was a distant flare.

"Scratch one ghost," Weapons said.

"There are others?"

"Only seven."

"Shoot them, too," Kirsty ordered.

"Aye, aye," said Weapons.

This time it was not so easy. The ghost images had begun a frantic dance of movement that flitted them from side to side in all directions, but one vector of their movement kept them coming toward the ship.

"Kirsty," Weapons said, "three down. The others are closing. I suggest we up shields."

"Can't. The launch is just ten minutes away from the lock," Kirsty said.

"That's going to be cutting it close. There's another wave of those things coming up out of atmosphere. I hate to be the one to tell you this, Lieutenant, but my guess is that we're under attack."

"The captain will be aboard in nine-minutes-five seconds. As soon as we have the launch inboard, we'll blink the hell out of here," Kirsty said.

"Erin Kenner," said Josh Webster's voice, "prepare to accept launch entry."

"Lock is open, Captain," Kirsty said.

Kirsty looked at Sheba and winked. "Don't you think I'm pretty cool under stress?"

"Magnificently so," Sheba said, with one of her blazing smiles.

"Inside I'm a quivering mass," Kirsty said. "Hurry, Captain, hurry."

The minutes were eternal until the ship vibrated ever so slightly with the landing of the launch in its cradle. Kirsty closed the outer hatch and lock, fed air into the cradle chamber. "Hold onto your stomach," she said, as she pushed in a blink that took the *Erin Kenner* six light-years away from DF-2.

"That's funny," Kirsty said.

"I'm not sure I want to know," Sheba said.

"The beacon we just planted is dead," Kirsty said.

"Kirsty," said Weapons in a high, excited voice, "we've got contact. Size and mass consistent with the ship we blasted back on DF-2."

"Hostile action?"

"Not at the moment."

"Get it in your sights and hold it there," Kirsty said. "If it so much as burps, blast it." She buzzed Engineering. "We're going to have to pick up that blink beacon and see what went wrong with it. Stand by to take it aboard."

There was only silence.

"Engineering?"

Silence.

Behind her the door to the corridor that led past the engineering cubicles to the launch cradle was flung open. She whirled. Her first impression was of overwhelming blackness from which glowed two glaring eyes, then she saw a head, an articulated neck, long, hinged arms extending toward her from a powerful armored torso. She screamed as icy, hard fingers dug into her shoulder, penetrating flesh, shattering bone. The other hand seized her under the chin and pulled. Her neck snapped and tendons tore. As she fell to the deck Sheba tried to run, but a second black, armored extension leapt with startling swiftness to block her way.

* * *

Sheba knew with chilling certainty that Josh was dead. On the deck Kirsty Girard was also dead, although her legs were jerking in ragged rhythm. The two things, machines, black demons, stood motionless, their glaring eyes unblinking.

She couldn't believe how calm she was. "Listen," she said, "whoever you are, whatever you are, listen. We did not come here to harm you or to disturb you in any way. We came looking for my mother and father and my sister and brother."

The extension that had killed Kirsty lifted one arm.

"You're going to kill me, too, aren't you?" Sheba asked.

There was only silence. The extension took one step forward, its metal foot brushing aside one of Kirsty's limp arms.

"It's all senseless," Sheba said. "We meant you no harm. The other members of my family meant you no harm."

Now both of the extensions moved slowly toward her.

"Just tell me why," she said, still eerily calm. "Why do you kill us when we came with no ill will?"

Suddenly she laughed. At first it was a thoroughly feminine, throaty sound, a sound that had and would for many years to come excite the libidos of men who watched her on holofilm. She laughed because she knew why she was calm. She was merely playing another scene. More than once she had faced fictional death in some holofilm drama, and this was nothing more than a continuation of her make-believe life.

But as the extensions moved closer, the laugh became brittle and shrill and then faded.

"Why?" she asked, as one black, hinged arm reached out to her. "Just tell me why."

The voice spoke in English, but it was flat and uninflected. "Let them sleep," the voice said, "for when they awaken, the universe will tremble."

She screamed just once. One of the extensions seized her arm, its sharp, metal fingers penetrating. Her pain was brief, however, for the other armored extension seized her head in both hands and simply ripped it away from her neck.

* * *

"This is Weapons. What the hell is going on?" One of the extensions left the bridge to seek out the voice. The other studied the controls for a few moments, pushed buttons, set the ship's computer to spewing out data regarding the drive and the ship's operations. Black, sharp fingers punched in calculations. The outside lock opened. Within minutes the ship extension floated into the lock with the *Erin Kenner*'s blink beacon clamped to its side. To make room it smashed into the ship's launch. In the control room the black extension punched instructions into the computer. The *Erin Kenner* blinked.

And, as had been calculated, she came out of nonspace in the heart of the nearest star. The insignificant mass of ship, extensions, and flesh both dead and alive became a part of the reaction in the nuclear furnace.

* * *

Inside the hull of the *Fran Webster* the tiny flux engine of the specimen container purred on, suspending the bin three feet above the deck. Two animated extensions soared to the site and nudged the other specimen container into the ship. Ice began to hide the exposed metal once more. The animated extensions returned to the chamber below the ice. The Watcher was busy for a time. The barren rock that had been exposed by the aliens' weapons took on a coating of ice. Alternate routes of communications had minimized the damage. All sensors were working at just under ninety percent efficiency. That level matched the Designers' age deterioration charts and was acceptable.

The Watcher waited. The only evidence to indicate that the *Erin Kenner* had ever been to DF-2, as the aliens called it, was the dead bodies of the captain and four crewmen inside the *Fran Webster*. The Watcher considered destroying both the bodies and the pieces of equipment from the *Erin Kenner*, but decided that the risk of bringing the attention of the government of Man to DF-2 was outweighed by the need to keep the bodies of members of the Webster family to lure that last link in the chain of necessary silencing within reach. Once the last member of the family was silent, the peace that had blessed the planet for millennia would return.

CHAPTER FOURTEEN

Sarah Webster de Conde raised her voice to emphasize a specific criticism of the chairman of the Educational Oversight Board. The screen of the voice recorder recognized the change in modulation and printed the words in boldface. She paused, consulted her notes before going on. She was dressed in a loose fitting jumpsuit. Her hair was hanging free. She was alone in the house and she was feeling just a bit sorry for herself, for Pete and the kids were at the local shopping pod watching Sheba as Miaree on a giant holo-film stage while she was spending her Sunday afternoon preparing still another speech to be delivered to still another assemblage of parents of T-Town schoolchildren.

There were times when she regretted having decided to enter politics. She liked people well enough, and enjoyed her moments in the spotlight, but the campaign was making unanticipated demands on her time. She hadn't yet resigned as leader of Cyd's Young Explorer group, but her assistant leader had been going it alone. Pete had hired a driver to chauffeur Petey and Cyd to dance class, Space Scouts, groundball practice, visits to friends. There were six million people in Tigian City and it seemed that all of them had children in school and wanted to hear Sarah de Conde's solutions to the problems that plagued the school system.

She was speaking about discipline. Her words appeared on the screen as she spoke. She was moderately well pleased with the way it was going. Most of the time she spoke without notes or rehearsal, but the speech on Monday night was especially important. At least a thousand parents from T-Town's most troubled district would be in the hall.

"Discipline is not punishment," she was saying when the screen went black and flashed her name.

SARAH. SARAH. SARAH. SARAH.

She shook her head in exasperation and reset the machine.

SARAH. SARAH.

"Oh, damn," she said. She pounded on the side of the screen.

HELP US, SARAH. HELP US.

The words were in boldface caps.

HELP US. HELP US.

She felt momentary panic, for in addition to the words on the screen there were images in her mind. Joshua and Sheba. David and Ruth. She leapt to her feet and turned the voice recorder off. A soft, musical chime announced that there was someone at the door. She touched the communicator on her desk.

"Yes, who is it, please?" she asked.

"My name is Vinn Stern," a pleasant male

voice said. "I'd like to speak with Mrs. de Conde. I'm a friend of Sheba Webster."

"One moment," she said. She switched on the front door viewer, saw a rather handsome, well dressed man. She opened the front door.

"Sorry to bother you on a Sunday afternoon, Mrs. de Conde," Vinn Stern said. "I just wanted to know if you've heard from Sheba in the last few months."

"No, I haven't," Sarah said. "Do you work with Sheba?"

"I was scientific adviser on her last picture," Vinn said.

Sarah sighed inwardly. First the voice recorder goes crazy, she thought, and now this. "You'd better come in, Mr. Stern."

"Thank you."

"May I offer you something?" she asked, as she led him into the rather sternly furnished room which Pete called his audience hall. The chairs were hard and uncomfortable, the decor stark. It was a room designed to encourage callers to state their business and seek more pleasant surroundings.

"No, thank you," Vinn said. He sat on the edge of a hard chair. Sarah sat primly, knees together, hands in her lap.

"I had assumed that Sheba was either at her home on Selbel or working somewhere on another film," Sarah said.

"She stowed away on her brother's X&A ship," Vinn said.

Sarah laughed. "That sounds exactly like

Sheba. Poor Joshua.'' She leaned forward. ''But you must tell me all about it.''

''We'd just finished the picture, *The Legend Of Miaree*. Captain Webster's ship arrived. They talked about your other brother and your sister, and your parents, of course, and Captain Webster told us that he was going out to look for them. When the ship left the planet where we'd been filming, Sheba disappeared, and I was pretty worried until I found a note pasted to the mirror in my bedroom stating that she was going to sneak aboard the *Erin Kenner*.''

''You and Sheba were—'' She left the question unfinished.

''Friends,'' he said. He grinned. ''I had the brass to hope that we could be more.'' He brushed back a forelock of thick, dark hair. ''Mrs. de Conde, I'm a bit anxious about her. It's been six months. The studio has not heard from her. I can't get much out of X&A, but they did condescend to tell me that the *Erin Kenner* was on routine exploration duty and, since she was in unexplored areas, there were no communication routes.''

''It is my impression that when an X&A explorer goes into new territory it leaves blink beacons behind it,'' Sarah said.

Sarah, Sarah, help us. Come.

She shook her head quickly.

''Yes,'' Vinn said.

''Mr. Stern, I don't think there's anything I can do.''

''Your husband is on the T-Town Board of Governors,'' Vinn said. ''He could reach a higher source at X&A.''

"Yes," she agreed. "Yes, I'll ask him to make inquiries. Are you staying in T-Town?"

He gave her the name of his hotel, rose. She offered her hand. "When I have something to tell you, I'll call you, Mr. Stern."

"I just hope that I'm not worrying you without reason," he said.

"No." She heard the voices, Josh's voice, Sheba's voice. *We need you, Sarah.* "It's time to be concerned, I think."

"Once again let me apologize for disturbing you on Sunday afternoon," Vinn said, as she walked him to the front door.

* * *

Sarah got lost twice in the labyrinthine corridors of X&A headquarters before she found the office of Staff Colonel Jefferson Watch. Pete's position and influence had secured an appointment quickly, but when she was shown into Watch's office by a polite Service rating she realized that Pete de Conde's request had not been given serious priority. Colonel Watch was a man in the middle fourth quarter of his life. Sarah knew enough about the Service to understand that she'd been steered to a man who was serving out his last few years before retirement, a man who had been pushed aside in the fierce competition for top command.

In spite of his wrinkles and white hair, Watch was an impressive man. He rose from his desk, a smile showing that he'd availed himself of the finest dentures available.

"Did you have a pleasant trip from Tigian, Mrs. de Conde?" he asked, as he shook her hand.

"I abhor space travel," Sarah said, answering his smile. "But as it goes, it was a pleasant enough trip I suppose."

"I think you'll find that chair comfortable," Watch said. "Coffee? Tea?"

"Neither, thank you."

He sat down behind his desk and picked up a folder emblazoned with the seal of X&A. "I have been going over the information given to me by fleet control," he said. "You are concerned about the *Erin Kenner,* commanded by Captain Joshua Webster?"

"My brother, Captain Webster, went into space searching for other members of my family who have been missing for some time. It has been just over two years since my mother and father were last reported."

"Ah, yes, the *Old Folks,* Tigian registry."

"And the *Fran Webster,* owned by my other brother, David Webster, went missing in the same segment of space about a year ago."

Watch cleared his throat. "Actually, Mrs. de Conde, the Service does not consider either of those two ships to be overdue. As you must know there are vast distances and huge star populations involved in any exploratory venture away from the established route. Your parents' ship, for example, still has almost one year's supplies, not counting the space rations which would last, in an emergency, for some months."

"Colonel Watch," she began.

He cut her off skillfully, with a smile. "If any

one of the ships about which you're concerned
had filed a flight plan stating that it would arrive
at some specific destination at some appointed
time, then there would be room for concern.
However, both *Old Folks* and the *Fran Webster*
filed an exploratory agenda for an indefinite period of time.''

She opened her mouth, but he held up his hand
to silence her. ''As for the *Erin Kenner,* I would
be highly surprised to hear from her inside of two
years from her departure from the U.P. Sector.
It's her job to seek out the lonely places.''

''Isn't it Service policy to leave behind permanent blink beacons when an exploratory ship is
charting new star lanes?''

''Yes, of course.''

''And isn't it standard operating procedure for
all X&A ships in the field to send back status reports once a month?''

''Under normal circumstances,'' Watch said.
''In fact, *Erin Kenner* sent back her routine position reports, including one from a new blink
beacon positioned in toward the core from the extragalactic route. We know, however, that it was
Captain Webster's intention to search a given area
for *Old Folks* and the *Fran Webster.* I don't know
whether you understand the complicated nature of
such a search, Mrs. de Conde. Let me give you
an example. Let us say, since the search area is
near the periphery of the galaxy, that it contains
only a few hundred stars within, say, a radius of
a hundred light-years. Many of those stars could
be eliminated because of their size and nature.
Say only a hundred of them were of the types

known to spawn planets. The *Erin Kenner* could work for a year or more and not have examined all of them, since approaching each new star would require weeks of short jumps and careful movements. During such an operation, which is essentially local, the ship would not be laying down permanent blink beacons and, therefore, she would be out of communications with headquarters.''

"I get the idea, Colonel, that it's going to be some time before X&A gets concerned about the situation."

"I sympathize with your wanting to have word of your relatives," he said. "And it is highly unusual, isn't it, to have so many members of the same family jumping about in the same region of space. I can only submit to you, Mrs. de Conde, that David and Ruth Webster acted impulsively. The search for *Old Folks* should have been left to Service professionals."

"The search for *Old Folks* and the *Fran Webster* is being conducted by a Service professional," she said. "And I know my brother, Josh. He's a stickler for regulations. I am convinced that he would not allow six months to go by without filing his reports with headquarters."

Watch cleared his throat again. "The *Erin Kenner* carries enough firepower to protect herself in any eventuality. Captain Webster, although this is his first command, has an excellent record." He stood in dismissal, his smile showing his gleaming dentures. "Don't worry, Mrs. de Conde. I'm sure that all of your family will turn up."

She had taken time from the middle of a closely

contested election campaign to make the trip to
Xanthos. She was fuming silently as she left Colonel Watch's office. She spent the night in a luxury hotel, but nothing pleased her. The food did
not sit well. The bed was too hard. In her dreams
they all called to her, Josh, David, Ruth, Sheba,
her mother and father.

She fretted on the shuttle that took her to Xanthos Space, a trip that lasted two hours longer than
the blink back to Tigian. She took a taxi to Pete's
office and arrived just in time for lunch. He saw
that she was upset and waited for her to pick her
own time to tell him about her trip. In the restaurant she toyed with a plate of fruit and salad while
her husband ate with gusto. She asked him about
developments in the election campaign, although
she'd only been gone overnight. Then, at the last,
she told him about Colonel Watch and the brushoff she'd been given at X&A Headquarters.

"I'm sorry," Pete said. He chuckled. "It's
rather deflating to know that my influence on Xanthos rates me an appointment with a passed-over
staff colonel counting the days until retirement."

"It's not your fault," Sarah said, putting her
hand on his. "You did all you could."

"Perhaps if I put on a little pressure here and
there we can do better than your Colonel Watch.
Both the central government and a Zede consortium are negotiating with us for the output of the
mines on that new planet out in the Two Sisters
quadrant. I'm patriotic, most of the time, but I
don't like to be treated like some yokel from Outworld Four."

"Forget it, Pete," she said. "Maybe Watch was

right. Maybe we're all being too impulsive. For the time being, I'm going to operate on the theory that if we leave them alone they'll all come home.''

''Wagging their tails behind them,'' Pete said with grin.

''I've got an election to win,'' she said.

''That Stern fellow called twice this morning to see if you were back.''

''I'll call him.''

''You don't suppose the Queen is serious about him?''

Sarah shrugged. ''With Sheba, who knows.'' She smiled. ''But it's about time for her to find a permanent attachment. I get a bit prickly reading about all of her romances in the media.''

Pete signaled the waiter, gave him his card, pulled back Sarah's chair. They parted outside the restaurant. Sarah went directly home and was hard at work on her speech when she remembered Vinn Stern. She punched in the number of his hotel. The call began to ring in his room.

''Sarah, please,'' Sheba's voice said.

She jerked back from the communicator.

''We need you, Sarah,'' Ruth said urgently. ''Don't ignore us like this.''

''Vinn Stern,'' a male voice said.

''Mr. Stern,'' Sarah said weakly.

''You're back.''

''With less than satisfactory news,'' she said. She went on to give him a full report.

''Vinn,'' said Sheba, ''listen to me, please. Help us. Help all of us.''

"That's a very good imitation of Sheba, Mrs. de Conde," Vinn said bitterly.

"Vinn, Sarah," Sheba said, "only you can help us. The two of you."

Sarah switched off the communicator with a shaking hand. "All right," she said. "That's it. That's all. I won't have any more. I am not insane and I don't intend to be. I am going to work on my speech, I'm going to give it, and for the next six weeks I'm going to campaign night and day."

In her mind there was a surprisingly vivid image of Sheba weeping.

"Damn it, Sheba," Sarah said loudly, looking around, "where are you?"

"You know," Sheba said. *"You know, Sarah."*

For six weeks Sarah was busy with hand-shakings and speeches and media interviews. She was willing to appear anywhere two or more people gathered who were interested in the state of T-Town's schools. She attended an awards ceremony for Petey's Space Scout troop and shook hands with all of the parents. She sent Frenc off on her camping trip. She talked half a dozen times with Vinn Stern. He was still in T-Town, for what reason Sarah couldn't imagine. She had begun to wonder if Vinn was just another of the hard-smitten fans who often made attempts to get close to Sheba.

In the last frenzied week she managed to put everything out of her mind. On election day she visited polling places and shook hundreds of hands. She lost the election by less than five thousand votes. Pete threw a "victory" party.

"My wife lost an election," he said, "but I won a wife."

The little gathering was at home. Their closest friends were there. When Vinn Stern showed up, Sarah was surprised.

"He seems to be so concerned about Sheba," Pete said. "I guess I felt sorry for him, so I invited him."

Vinn didn't get a chance to talk with Sarah alone until late in the evening. Sarah had celebrated with three glasses of a very fine Selbelese wine.

"I was sorry to hear that you lost the election by such a close margin," Vinn said.

"As opposed to losing it by a large margin?" she asked.

He laughed. "If my speech is a bit imprecise, blame it on your husband. He keeps insisting that I sample still another new wine."

"I feel a bit imprecise myself," Sarah admitted. "As for losing, the professional politicians told me that they were amazed that I did so well. They say that if I continue to work hard for the next four years I'll be sure of election next time."

"And?" he asked, raising one eyebrow.

"Four years is a long time and I have three kids to raise."

"I'm sure you'll do a splendid job of it," he said. "Look, can we talk?"

"About what?" she asked, although she knew what he meant.

He looked at her intently. "It wasn't you imitating Sheba that day on the communicator."

"No."

"Do you hear her voice often?"

"Yes." Had it not been for the wine she would not have admitted it. "You?"

"Constantly. Ever since I came to Tigian City."

"And not before that?" she asked.

"No."

She mused over that information for a moment, then smiled. "Well, if I'm going crazy, so are you," she said. "It's impossible, you know, this business of Sheba—and the others—speaking to me—to us—across time and space."

"But she does," Vinn said with intensity, leaning toward her. "I can't help but believe that she's in serious trouble."

"There's nothing we can do," Sarah said.

"I have been in contact with a mercenary," he said. "He owns a reconditioned scout. Not big, but well rigged and well armed."

"Don't," she said quickly. "Three ships missing in the same volume of space are enough."

"I love Sheba, Mrs. de Conde."

"Yes, I know," she said, lulled away from any suspicion of him by his obvious sincerity. "And how does Sheba feel about you?"

He spread his hands. "She seems to like me."

"Still—"

"Mrs. de Conde, I want you to understand how desperate I am to ask you this. Chartering a mercenary ship is expensive, and I'm a man who lives on a salary—of which there isn't one at the moment. One way or the other I'm going out there."

"It's a big galaxy," she said.

"But not big enough for me to get away from her voice begging me to help."

"I know."

"Will you help me?" he asked.

She was silent for long seconds. "Yes. How much?"

"Fifty thousand credits."

"Well, I can't take that much out of the household accounts. I'll have to talk with Pete."

"Will you, please?"

* * *

"Fifty thousand credits is pretty steep," Pete said. "I can private charter one of the company ships for half that price."

"A freighter?" Sarah asked.

"An executive liner," he said.

"Mr. Stern sets great store by the fact that the mercenary ship is well armed."

"Our Zede subsidiaries believe in going armed," Pete said. "I can charter one of their mining exploration ships. It'll be equipped with anything Mr. Stern thinks might be necessary."

"Thank you for not laughing at me," Sarah said.

"I would never do that." He took her hand. "I've been watching you, my dear. You're a bit off your feed. You're losing weight, and I like you just the way you are."

"The election," she said.

"No. You thrive on that kind of pressure. My guess is that it's the worry about your family."

"I do worry."

"Well, tell your Mr. Stern that I'll order a Zede vessel in here as quickly as one can be made available.'' He scratched his chin. ''On second thought, send him to see me so that we can discuss armament and other needs. He's quite a fellow, you know. Science boffin. Big brain. He's mainly a computer type, but he's been around. Did some time with X&A weapons development when he was first out of university.''

''I didn't know.''

''Since we can't send the *Rimfire* and the whole fleet out, I guess sending Stern is our best bet to ease your mind about your folks.''

''Thank you, Pete.''

He grinned. ''Well, you ought to know that even after all the years we've been married all you have to do is ask.''

''I have one more request,'' she said.

''Shoot.''

''I want to go with Mr. Stern.''

He chewed on his lower lip for long moments. ''All right,'' he said. ''We need a vacation.''

''We?''

''You don't think I'm going to send my sexy wife off alone into space with a handsome stud like this Stern fellow.''

''I don't want to take you away from your work.''

''Don't worry about it. Listen, my old man used to tell me, 'Pete, there's nothing more important in this life than looking after your own.' All of my people are dead, but your folks are mine by marriage, and they're important to me not only because I like them, but because you love them.'' He came around the desk and kissed her lightly.

"Now get the hell out of here so I can put in a call to the Zede office. Go get packed or something. Don't forget to put in my motion sickness pills. You know how I hate it when a ship blinks."

CHAPTER FIFTEEN

Many natives of the fifty-plus Zede System worlds were romantics who styled themselves as being more sensitive to love, life, beauty, and esthetics in general than the somewhat benighted denizens of the hustle-bustle worlds of the mainstream United Planets society. This pose did not prevent Zedians from developing efficient industry and cutting edge technology. As David Webster had known, ownership of a Zede Starliner marked a man as being tasteful and, not coincidentally, quite rich; but luxury liners were just one aspect of Zede leadership. The Verbolt Cloud chamber, the heart of all modern computers, was a Zede development. The descendants of Jonathan Blink, inventor of the blink drive that sent man to the stars, had settled on a Zede world during the diaspora from New Earth and the name was still alive in the system.

Whether a Zedian was poetic or practical, a practitioner of the cultural arts or a machinist, he was possessed of an adamant pride. The Zede worlds, he would say—and loudly—were the most beautiful, the most fruitful, the most cultured, the most technologically developed.

Genealogy was and had always been important to a Zedian. It was an ancestorally impoverished man who couldn't trace his lineage back to the colonial period, with a significant emphasis on those of his forebears who had fought and died in the thousand year old Zede War. That ancient conflict had left scars both on the Zedian national character and in Zedian space. Tour ships ran regular schedules to the areas of scattered asteroids that had once been blue planets, water planets, life zone planets.

A true citizen of a Zede world forget that once ships from the U.P. proper had sent planet busters blasting down into verdant, fertile worlds? Never. The old battle flag of the Zede League was still being manufactured and sold by the millions, and, as the Zede mining exploration ship *Carmine Rose* blinked away from Tigian toward the rim of the galaxy, that familiar Zede symbol was painted on her bow in vivid reds and blacks.

The ship looked like anything but its colorful namesake. She was squat and angular, built for doing a tough job under the harsh conditions of space rather than for beauty. Brutally efficient tools for digging, boring, blasting, and sampling made odd little nodules on her hull; and to the eye of an experienced spaceman the ports and protrusions of her weapons systems were quite evident.

In spite of her hard-nosed exterior her interior offered not just comfort for her crew of two and their three passengers, but a surprising degree of luxury. She was, then, a typical product of Zede genius, tough and let's-get-it-done on the outside, a pussycat inside. She had the same power plant that had been developed for the new fleet class space tugs and the conveniences of a passenger liner. She was legally the property of a subsidiary of Pete de Conde's primary corporation, but she was in the care of, and was the pride, joy, and only child of Iain and Kara Berol, loyal and poetically practical citizens of the Zede world, Haven.

Iain Berol was a large man, barrel shaped, strong-necked, and powerful. He wore his hair long and shaggy. In contrast to his percheron body his face was almost delicate, with a strong, straight nose, smoldering black eyes, and chiseled chin. His wife, Kara, was built to match, a big girl, but formed as gracefully and as curvaceously as a sports flyer. She had a pixieish smile that, when properly applied, lit not only her face but a considerable area surrounding her. Kara was pilot and navigator. She could make the *Rose*'s Phase II computer do everything but tap dance and sing songs. Iain was weapons man, general technician, drive engineer, and mining expert. He took it on himself to be the prime host to the passengers, among whom was the H.M.F.I.C. in charge of a business empire encompassing the mining company that owned the *Carmine Rose*.

There were no complaints from the passengers, although both Mr. and Mrs. de Conde confined themselves to their cabin for a period which lasted through the first half dozen blinks. The third passenger, Vinn Stern, showed great curiosity about the ship. He had endless questions for Kara Berol about the drive, the mining equipment, and the weaponry. Once the *Rose* was out-galaxy and blinking along the *Rimfire* route Vinn offered to stand watch. Kara, who hated six-on-six-off watches, readily agreed. She told Iain that Vinn was fully capable of taking a full eight hour watch. The major portion of each watch consisted of enduring the long charging periods after *Rose* had drained her generator in the swift coverage in multiple jumps of a few hundred light-years; and since the *Rimfire* route was so well delineated even a neophyte navigator such as Vinn could tune the blinkstat communicator to the next beacon, copy the coordinates onto the computer, and push a button.

While on duty Vinn spent his time familiarizing himself with *Rose*'s very interesting systems. She was, he found, one hell of a well equipped ship. Kara told him that *Rose*'s detection instruments matched those aboard an X&A fleet cruiser. Her weapons were awesome. Her computer was the latest Zede development, a Phase II model that Vinn had not seen. After having become acquainted with the computer's slight differences and peculiarities, Vinn decided that the Zede machine was not superior in general function to the standard Century series that was in use on U.P. ships, but it did have minor features that offered him interesting little challenges. In addition to the inaccessible area wherein resided X&A's little black box—the "spy box," as Kara called it—another area of memory was closed off to the noninformed user. It took Vinn five watches to break into the closed file. It listed, defined, and gave operating instructions for the *Carmine Rose*'s weapons system. That in itself was not surprising. The startling thing was that the *Rose* was even better armed than Vinn had dreamed.

"Pete," Vinn asked as soon as he had opportunity to be alone with de Conde, "did you know that this ship carries two planet busters?"

"Damn, Vinn," Pete said in surprise.

"You didn't?"

Pete scratched his nose.

De Conde's hesitation to answer was revealing. "You did know," Vinn said.

"I'm wondering how in hell you found out," Pete said. He scratched his nose again.

"One of my assignments when I worked on Xanthos was to develop methods to search out hidden files," Vinn said. "And when I'm alone with a computer I lose all self-control and can't keep my hands off it." He grinned, then sobered. "Why the illegal weapons, Pete?"

"It depends on where you are and how you look at the question whether or not they're legal," de Conde said. "Somewhere way to hell and gone out in the big empty where no X&A ship has ever gone there's no one to say they're not allowed."

Vinn knew and he knew that Pete knew that busters were forbidden to any vessel, anywhere. "You haven't told me why you need them," he said.

De Conde looked away. "Well, I suppose a buster could be considered a mining tool under certain circumstances."

"Damn," Vinn said. "I believe you're going to tell me that your company has used them in the past."

"Not lately." Pete grinned. "The last time was

about ten years ago. The system was isolated. There was a big, airless moon orbiting a gas giant. It was a useless hunk of rock, except that it had a core of metals so pure that it was almost unnecessary to refine them.''

''You blew a moon apart?''

''A lot easier to mine that way,'' Pete said.

''My God,'' Vinn said. ''If X&A knew— Hell, if they knew that this ship had been within twenty light-years of Xanthos with two busters aboard—''

Pete chuckled. ''But they don't.'' He put his hand on Vinn's arm. ''Look, Vinn, we have the tightest security in the galaxy. You take Iain and Kara. They've been submitted to every psychological test ever devised, and it's our policy to pay key employees enough to make them not just loyal but fanatic. They own shares in the company. They're as solid as people can be. We damned sure wouldn't want a couple of unstable nuts running around with two busters aboard.''

Vinn ran his hand through his hair. ''Well, you said this ship would be well armed.''

It took Vinn another few watches to puzzle out the complicated firing sequence for the planet busters. The process was even more of a challenge than breaking Kara's code to get into the file in the first place. It helped pass the long hours of charging time. He was working out the last sequence one day when Sarah came into control and looked over his shoulder. She asked questions. At first Vinn hedged, then he decided that she had a right to know.

She paled when he told her. "This ship could destroy a world?" she asked.

"Two of them."

"There are safeguards, of course."

"The firing orders are quite complicated."

"Show me."

"It's not that I don't trust you, Sarah, but one of the safeguards is that it takes both Iain and Kara to arm and fire one of the weapons," he said.

"But you're able to defeat the fail-safes?"

He shrugged. "I've spent a lot of time with these things. I'd say that there aren't more than half a dozen people in the U.P. who could break the entry code and dope out the steps it takes to send one of those things zapping toward a planet." He grinned wryly. "Don't intend to brag. It's just that I think in computerese."

"You could launch one of those things all by yourself?"

"If necessary," he said. "I can't imagine any sequence of events that would cause me to do it, though."

"It gives me the shivers," she said.

"You are not alone," he said, as he overrode the commands that had brought him within three steps of having one of the planet destroying weapons ready to fire. "By the way, if it's all the same to you I'd just as soon Iain and Kara don't know I busted into private areas."

The *Carmine Rose* made a left turn relating to the plane of the galactic disc and jumped inward to the one permanent blink beacon laid down by the *Erin Kenner*. There she paused, while those aboard her gathered in the control room and studied the sparse sprinkling of stars that lay within a relatively few light-years.

"Here's where the fun begins," Kara Berol said. "Offhand I'd guess that we have six months' work ahead of us just checking out the nearest stars."

But there was a Webster aboard, and, like Ruth and Sheba before her, Sarah Webster de Conde remembered her mother's shopping habits. So it was that the *Carmine Rose* followed the same procedures that had led three other ships carrying Websters to the ice planet.

Those who studied the human brain and mind had long since negated the myth of racial memory. The experts were in agreement, however, that the actions and attitudes of a people could be affected by their legends. A Zedian had, somewhere in his subconscious mind, the semi-memory of dying worlds. Therefore, in unknown space, a Zedian ship's captain, such as Iain Berol, often took precautions that would have made the most meticulous X&A commander seem reckless. As the *Rose* approached the planet, she bristled with weapons at the ready, and she sent out an electronic cacophony of detection signals.

Kara Berol, at instrument control, pointed out to the others, first of all, the total lack of life signals and electromagnetic radiation from the icy world. This precautionary survey completed, she turned herself to other tests.

"What we have here is a round ice cube with a hot core," she said. "The depth of the ice cover ranges from roughly two hundred feet to several miles in the ocean basins, where the density of the deep ice shows salinity."

Iain, at weapons control, was scanning for metal. "Boss," he said, "I think we'd better file a claim as soon as we can. This one has good ore fields, light metals to heavy."

"Wouldn't that have been the first thought of anyone else who took the same readings?" Vinn asked.

Iain frowned. "To answer that you have to assume that the other ships came here."

Kara was bent over her instrument panel, her fingers busy at the detection station keyboard. Suddenly she straightened. "I think you all had better take a look at this," she said.

She displayed the findings of a surface scan. On the screen the regular pattern of metallic installations extended to the horizons of the world that turned slowly beneath them.

"What we should do, right now, is jump back to the beacons and yell loudly for an X&A alien contact ship," Kara said.

Pete de Conde said, "If I had always done what I should have done, at least according to the rules, I'd still be crunching numbers in an accounting office." He turned to Iain. "There's nothing living down there? Nothing to indicate any sort of activity?"

"None," Iain said.

Pete took Sarah's hand. "We came out here to find your family," he said. "Do you want to go back now?"

"I don't want to endanger the ship, nor anyone in her," Sarah said.

"I see no harm in taking a few more readings," Vinn said.

"I'm thinking of a share of discoverer's rights when the mining crews go to work out here," Kara said, lighting the room with her happy smile.

"Kara, set us up in a polar orbit so that we'll cover the whole surface," Vinn said. He lifted one hand. "Sorry, I didn't mean to sound as if I was giving orders."

"No problem," Kara said, her fingers flying as she punched in the problem. A few quick bursts of flux power positioned the *Rose* into the desired orbit. Instruments charted the surface. Pete and Sarah left control to have a meal and a rest. Iain was alert, watching the detectors diligently. Kara was monitoring the viewer as the grid of regularly shaped metal objects was charted. Vinn was using the most powerful of the optics to examine the surface.

"Oh, ho," Kara said.

"What? What?" Vinn asked.

She read off figures to indicate a specific spot on the surface. Vinn focused the optics on a mound of ice that protruded slightly above the level plain.

"See anything interesting?" Kara asked.

"Something on the surface. It's not covered as thickly as its surroundings."

"Durametal," Kara said.

Vinn felt his heart flip. "Program for stationary orbit," he said.

"Aye, aye."

Holding her position directly over the mass of durametal, *Rose* used all of her sensors and detectors. "There are two separate objects," Kara said. "The mass of one matches that of a Mule, the other a Zede Starliner."

Iain said, "It's decision time, kiddies."

Vinn chewed on his lower lip, thinking of Sheba. They couldn't know for sure, not just yet, but it was odds on that the two durametal objects under a shallow coating of ice were *Old Folks* and David's Starliner. "Iain, before we call Pete and Sarah in for a conference, let's complete the surface sweep."

"I can understand how civilians might disregard standard procedure and land on an untested planet," Iain said, "but I don't think you're going to find an X&A explorer down there."

"Resuming polar orbit," Kara said.

They did not, of course, find an X&A ship on the surface of the planet. They found only more of the grid installations. Twenty-four hours later, the planetary sweep completed, *Rose* floated in stationary orbit above the two durametal objects. A port opened. A small, projectile-shaped drone fluxed away toward the surface.

The drone represented Zede technology at its best. It was thought controlled. Kara wore the control helmet. As the probe reached the icy mound on the surface, she projected the probe's binocular vision images onto a screen. The little vessel hovered, sent out a beam of heat. Durametal was quickly exposed. Kara shifted the drone's position and the heat beam penetrated the open lock of a Zede Starliner.

Sarah held her breath as the optics of the probe took them inside the hull of the ice-bound ship.

"Look at this," Kara said, zooming in on a specimen container that hovered on flux two feet above the icy deck.

"How long would the power last in that flux engine?" Iain asked.

"Just over a year," Vinn said. "Kara, can you clear away the frost there on the front of that bin?"

The probe flared heat, and he knew that Sheba was dead, for the ice melted to show the X&A logo, and, under it, the name *Erin Kenner*. The specimen bin had belonged to Joshua's ship. He felt heavy. He wanted nothing more than to be alone, to grieve for what might have been. But Kara, in grim silence, had moved the probe to scan the control room of the starliner. There were four bodies on the deck. Through the film of ice came a definite tinge of Service blue.

"You might not want to see this, Sarah," Kara said, as she positioned the probe and focused. The frozen face looked up at them with an expression of surprise.

"Oh, Josh," Sarah whispered. "Oh, please, no."

"That's your brother?" Iain asked.

Pete put his arm around Sarah. "Yes," he said. "That's Joshua Webster."

"What's in the bins?" Iain asked.

"Let's have a look," Kara said.

It took a while, after the probe was positioned above the bin, to make out the mass inside. Kara played the heat beam lightly over the frozen contents. Ruth Webster's face emerged, ruptured eyeballs looking upward past a male head.

It took some time to discover the second specimen bin, which had been left outside when Josh and his party entered the Fran Webster.

"They are all here," Sarah said weakly, when she recognized the ruined faces of her mother and father. "All except Sheba."

"So now we know," Iain said. "Is it time to call in the shock troops?"

"I'm going to take Sarah to our cabin," Pete said.

"That wasn't an answer, was it?" Kara asked, after the de Condes were gone.

"I'm feeling a small suggestion of outright panic," Iain said.

"Pete de Conde didn't get to be one of the richest men in the U.P. by following the letter of the rules," Kara said.

"I'm going to bring up the probe," Iain said.

"No," Vinn said sharply.

"Huh?" said Iain.

"There are eight bodies down there," Vinn said. "And we have no idea what happened to the *Erin Kenner* and the rest of her crew."

"That machine represents a lot of credits," Iain said. "And I'm signed for it."

"Leave it. Park it. Maybe we can retrieve it later."

"Leave it, Iain," Kara said. "He's right. We don't know what we're dealing with here."

"I want no physical contact with the surface, either direct or secondhand, not until we know a lot more."

Iain bristled, but subsided. He'd had not a few conversations with Vinn during the trip out, and he knew that Vinn had good credentials. "All right," he said, "what's your suggestion?"

"Run all the tests again, and any others that we can think of."

"Polar orbit?" Kara asked.

"Please, Kara," Vinn said.

The monotonous task of scanning the entire surface of the planet again. Iain took a sleep break, leaving Kara on weapons and Vinn watching the instruments. The long hours passed.

"Do you mind if I have a look at the planet's magnetic field?" Vinn asked.

"Not at all," Kara said. "Punch in magnoscan."

"I think I know the procedure," Vinn said, his fingers flying over the keyboard.

There was nothing unexpected about the planet's magnetic field. A series of solar flares were sending strong flows of radiation into the thin atmosphere. Vinn measured the power of the flares and the intensity of the auroral display at the north pole. He used the computer's files to compare the readings to those of other planets and found nothing out of the ordinary.

Rose's instruments located an area of relatively thin ice which covered a broad, flat zone lacking the gridded metallic installations. Kara investigated.

"Hey, Vinn," she called out, "this empty area was hit by no less than three blasts from a laser cannon within the last year."

"The *Erin Kenner*," Vinn said.

"That's my guess, too," Kara said.

"Anything else?"

"Nope. No metal directly under the blast area. At least not enough to show on the ore field detectors. Whoever shot up the joint was using full power, because destruction was complete."

It was, it seemed, another blind lead, another dead end. Vinn looked at the viewscreen moodily. His fingers rested lightly on the keyboard. He sent out another search for life signals and there was nothing. Idly he punched in an order for detection of gravitational waves. That test hadn't been run previously because the duration and strength of the waves could be readily predicted by measurement of the planet's density, mass, and position in relationship to other solar system bodies. He was looking at the screen with only half of his attention, his thoughts once again with Sheba. It is human to hope, and he was trying desperately to abandon the mindset that she was dead.

At first he didn't realize what he was seeing. In addition to the image and measurements of standard gravitational waves there was a connected grid of waves covering the surface of the planet. Directed gravitational force joined each of the metallic installations of the grid.

"Vinn, what is it?" Kara asked, as he bent forward in obvious agitation.

"I don't know," he said. What he was seeing was impossible. While it was true that gravity could be created artificially aboard ship and nullified by the flux engine, it was not possible to direct such forces in straight lines, as was obviously being done under the ice of the planet.

Someone or something was vectoring gravity waves as power or communications or both. The implications of such advanced technology made the hair stand up on the back of his neck.

CHAPTER SIXTEEN

Pete de Conde sipped a cup of coffee as he stared at the grid pattern on the large screen. "Vinn, you're telling me that someone down there has found a way to direct the force of gravity along a single vector?"

"It looks that way," Vinn said, as he waited for the computer to print up the conclusion of a long and involved calculation. He was trying to figure the relative intensity of one of the straight lines of gravitational force that connected the metallic installations. In relation to the planetary force the answer involved one heck of a lot of zeros after a decimal point. But that figure was misleading, for it measured only the size of the gravitational increment represented by the line of direction and not the applied force or the energy equivalent.

"Then even though all of our instruments show that there's nothing down there under the ice there is, in effect, a live power grid covering the whole planet?" Pete asked.

"Power, or communication, or something I can't even imagine," Vinn said. "This is virgin territory for me."

"And for anyone else," Iain Berol said.

Pete rubbed his chin, sipped his coffee thoughtfully. "Those square constructions are refrigerating units," he said.

Vinn nodded. "That would seem to be the case."

"When someone shot up a few of them, the ice melted," Pete said. "Then the grid was reformed." He pointed to the area where there was a blank space in the regular grid of square installations. "See how the lines connecting the units are more distinct on all sides of the blank area? More power is being directed to those units, but even that isn't enough to reform the ice burden to its original depth. It's only a few feet thick there on the plain."

"But why put a whole planet in deep freeze?" Kara asked.

"Because they have something to hide," Pete said. "And they're willing to be nasty to keep it hidden."

"You keep saying 'they,' " Kara said. "But we get no life signals."

"Could your instruments detect life through several hundred feet of ice, frozen earth, and rock?" Pete asked.

"Through ice, yes," Kara said, "but only through a very shallow layer of earth and rock."

"So there could be something down there at a depth of several hundred feet below the surface," Pete said. "Something or someone who knows how to use gravity as power." He winked at Iain. "Iain, I wonder what the captain's discovery share would be if the *Carmine Rose* took home the secret of a new and unlimited source of cheap power?''

Iain whistled.

''Don't even think it, Pete,'' Vinn said. ''There are eight bodies down there and an X&A ship is missing. We're going to let the big boys handle this.''

''Son,'' Pete said, ''no brag, but I am one of the big boys. And this is my ship. Now whatever it is down there, whether it's a them or an it, it has killed off my wife's family. I think it owes her something for that. What do you say, Iain?''

''As you said, it's your ship.'' Iain grinned. ''I'm still trying to figure my discovery share of applied gravitational power.''

''Kara?'' Pete asked.

''I'm with Iain.''

''Do I have a vote?'' Sarah asked.

''Of course,'' Pete said.

''I would like to know what it was that killed my parents and my brothers and sisters.''

''And you're willing to risk the life of one more Webster, not to mention mine, to find out?'' Vinn asked.

Sarah looked thoughtful. ''I think,'' she said slowly, ''that if it could kill at a distance it would have killed us already. I know that it can reach out and touch me at a long distance. I think that whatever it is down there is able to get into my mind, because the very idea of me, Sarah Webster, being out here so far from home, from my children, from all of my involvements, cannot be explained without postulating some outside influence. I've been thinking a lot about that since we left Tigian. Vinn, it was entirely out of character for me to let you, a stranger, into my house when I was home alone. I had no urgent reason to believe that anything was wrong with any member of my family. My parents told us when they left that they might be gone for years. There was no crucial reason for David and Ruth to go jumping off looking for Mom and Dad—unless that idea was implanted by an outside force, and I know that they would never have done—what they were doing—on their own.''

She paused, looked into Vinn's eyes. ''You were in love with Sheba, Vinn, and so, naturally, she was on your mind, but why were you so convinced that she was in danger and needed your help?''

''I don't know,'' Vinn said.

''You heard her voice.''

He nodded. ''Yes, but I was so much in love—''

''I heard, too,'' Sarah said. ''You accused me of doing an imitation of Sheba.''

Vinn nodded grimly. He looked at the grid that was connected by the pinpoint lines of gravitational force.

''In theory, the gravitational force of this planet extends forever,'' he said. ''It's here and it's everywhere else at the same time. It would, of course, be distorted by other bodies, but it reaches the far end of the universe, even though its strength diminishes with distance.''

''It's quite a jump from here to the home planets,'' Iain said. ''If something down there did influence you two over that distance, was it using the gravitational waves of the planet as a carrier band, for lack of a better description?''

Vinn shrugged. ''Could be, but that doesn't explain how it could pinpoint one individual out of billions.''

''Why don't we leave the answers to that to the boffins?'' Pete asked. ''Are we agreed that there's something alive down there?''

''That depends on your definition of life,'' Vinn said. He didn't elaborate, but he had begun to form a definite idea about the nature of the intelligence that inhabited the ice planet. The others were silent, waiting.

''My bet is that it can't touch us up here,'' Pete said. ''I think Mom and Pop Webster got excited when they recorded all of the metallic readings and landed on the surface where they could be affected.''

''I can buy that,'' Vinn said. ''I can also accept the premise that David and Ruth Webster were lured down to the surface by the discovery of their parents' ship, but Joshua Webster was Service, making it difficult to explain why he was down there where it—or they—could get at him.''

''It reaches into the mind,'' Sarah said.

''If it can reach into the mind,'' Pete said, ''it can communicate with us.'' He winked at Iain. ''I'd like to talk with it about the manipulation of gravity. Why don't we try to open a dialogue?''

''What do you suggest?'' Iain asked.

''So far it's been ignoring us. Let's see if we can't force some kind of a reaction,'' Pete said. ''Iain, fire up the laser and cut the communication lines between a couple of those icing units.''

"You're forgetting the *Erin Kenner*," Vinn said. "Apparently she used force, blasting a few of the units. Did her use of force provoke greater force in return?"

"I am in agreement with the idea that if it could kill us while we're in space it would have done so already," Pete said. "Let's give my suggestion a try."

Vinn remembered Sheba's smile, the smell of her, the soft and warm feel of her in his arms. He nodded.

A laser beam lashed down and, like a surgical scalpel, slashed a narrow, deep cut into the ice directly over one of the connecting lines of force. Iain, at weapons control, monitored his sensors alertly.

"Ah, ha," Pete said, for instantly the intensity of the lines of force connecting the two separated units to others were reinforced as power was increased to bypass the severed line.

"Isolate that one unit," Pete said.

The beam flashed down, one, two, three times. One unit was completely cut off from all others. Within minutes a film of melt water appeared in the affected area as the sun's energy was absorbed by the ice.

"Kara," Iain said, his voice tense, "stand by for maneuver. Program a blink and stand by."

"Got it," Kara said, obeying without question.

"You wanted a response, boss," Iain said. "Take a look at screen two."

No less than half a dozen ships were lifting from the surface of the planet from different locations.

"Life search, Kara," Iain ordered.

"Negative, negative," Kara said, a few seconds later. "You're not going to believe this. Those ships have hydrogen fusion engines."

"Damned small plants, then," Vinn said. "They must take up most of the room aboard."

"Room for a few of those," Iain said, as a shower of missiles were launched from the climbing ships.

"Can you handle all of those?" Vinn asked nervously.

"Sure. It's just a matter of whether we want to blast them or evade them," Iain said. "If that's all our friend down there has, its weaponry doesn't match the feat of deep freezing a whole world. I can take the missiles out or blink away and let them blast on into empty space."

"And the ships?" Pete asked.

"I think that we can safely assume that they're hostile," Iain said.

"I think so," Pete said.

"I'm going to take one out," Iain said.

The long-range saffer beam exploded into brilliance as it entered the planet's thin atmosphere, but the flare of destruction as it contacted the leading attacker was brighter.

"I think that it's time you gave your attention to the missiles," Kara said. "If they carry nuclear warheads—and that seems logical since they're using a fusion power plant—we don't need to have them being detonated anywhere nearby."

"Got you," Iain said, and for the next forty seconds the ship shivered and rocked with the launching of counter missiles. Below, in the thin atmosphere, flowers of destruction blossomed.

"Shields up," Kara said, as a glow of light came from a ship that was still climbing out of the planet's gravity well.

"Laser?" Vinn asked.

"Limited range," Iain said. "I'm going to have to take out the other ships before they get closer. The shields would hold, I'm sure, but I'm not in the mood to take chances."

"I agree," Vinn said.

The saffer beam glowed. One by one the small vessels flared and disintegrated.

"Did anyone pinpoint the launch sites?" Vinn asked.

"All launch sites recorded," Kara said.

"Let's have a look at one."

The optics showed a rapidly closing hole in the surface ice. "Iain," Vinn asked, "can you use the saffer on lower power to melt a neat hole through to the surface just where that missile rested?"

"Consider it done," Iain said.

When the ice was melted and the water evaporated away, a closed, circular hatch was exposed.

"Want a look inside?" Iain asked.

"If you please, sir," Vinn said.

"Takes a delicate touch," Iain said, adjusting the saffer beam.

Metal went molten, sparkled away into the thin air. There was a flare of fire.

"Oxygen atmosphere inside," Iain said.

"Curious," Vinn said. "The spacecraft was unmanned, but came from an oxygen environment."

"We will talk," Sarah said.

"What?" Pete asked.

"Now we will talk," Sarah repeated, her voice flat and unemotional.

"Sarah?" Vinn asked, leaping up to put his hand on her arm.

She looked at Vinn and nodded. "It wants to talk," she said.

A soft gong rang and the computer's monitor came to life. Words formed quickly on the screen.

"Further destruction is not desirable."

Kara's fingers flew. "Who are you?"

"It is not necessary."

"What?" Kara asked.

"It is not necessary."

"It is not necessary for me to use the keyboard?" Kara asked.

"Affirmative."

"Who are you?" Vinn asked.

"I am that which was created."

"By whom?" Vinn asked.

"By the Creators."

"Why have you killed?" Sarah asked. She leaned forward, waiting for the answer to appear on the computer's screen.

"Let them sleep, for when they awaken the universe will tremble."

"You didn't answer my question, damn you," Sarah said. "Why did you kill my family?"

"I watch."

"And murder," Sarah whispered.

"Now we will talk."

"We are ready to talk," Vinn said. "Tell us why it was necessary for you to kill."

"I did not yet know that the time had come."

"What time has come?" Pete asked sharply.

"The time to talk."

The screen flickered. An image of the surface formed and as they watched ice shattered, cracked, parted to reveal a gray metal surface. Like a lens opening a circular cavity appeared. Words were superimposed over the image.

"You will come."

"What happened to the vessel called the *Erin Kenner*?" Vinn asked.

The image of the local sun, showing a series of flares reaching hungrily into space, appeared on the screen.

"A woman was aboard, a woman with long blonde hair and green eyes."

Vinn's heart pounded as an image of Sheba came to the screen to be consumed instantly by a blast of white.

"Why?" Sarah cried.

The images were in their minds. Among a field of closely crowded stars swam planets that, from a distance, showed the most wonderful color ever seen from the emptiness of space, the blue of a water world. A closer view of one planet showed the brown and green of continents, the feathery pattern of weather systems, the wide blue of oceans. With dizzying swiftness the viewpoint closed to show the graceful towers of a city. Vehicles crawled along the streets, soared through the sky. It was not possible to distinguish the details of tiny figures on the walks and the streets, but it was apparent that they walked on two legs. The towers were painted in bright, complementary colors, and the architectural styling was delicate.

Suddenly the spires that reached into the sky trembled, crumbled. Structures twisted, imploded. The crawling vehicles and the tiny figures were buried by falling debris. Flying vehicles fell from the sky to smash into the chaos. A longer view showed a storm of fire consuming the green forests. A pall of dust and smoke hid the world for long seconds and then, events having been obviously accelerated, they saw a barren globe. Even the atmosphere had been burned away. Everything on the surface had been reduced to rubble so small that no tiny piece could give a clue as to its origin.

There were other dead worlds. They were displayed one by one and then there was a moment of silence in the control room of the *Crimson Rose*.

The computer screen glowed. "I watch to assure that it will never happen again."

"You're right, it's time for us to talk," Vinn said.

"Come, then."

"When our friends came to you, you killed them," Vinn said.

"I did not know then that you were they who will come."

"We'll talk as we are talking," Vinn said. "At least for a while. What you've shown us happened long ago. You are old. Things are not as they once were. We are a peaceful people."

"You go armed."

"Yes, because we've seen the dead worlds," Vinn said. "Yes, because the universe is so vast and we know only a miniscule portion of our own galaxy. If we didn't go armed, we'd be dead now at your hands.''

"You are not dead. You are they who have come.''

"And you are—" Vinn did not put the concept into words. He pictured a core, a regularly spaced grid, and into his mind came corrections. The central storage areas of the Watcher were compact, occupying no more than three cubic yards of space inside a shell of force constructed of shaped gravitational waves. The ganglia of the Watcher's nervous system extended around the globe and were connected not only to the icing units but to hundreds of launch sites occupied by small ships, to an array of sensor and detection instruments. One large area was a blank in the image projected by the Watcher.

"You still have something to hide from us," Vinn said.

"You must know all, for you are they who have come.''

Once again the iris opened on the surface. This time a blaze of light flared upward, lighting a metal-lined chamber.

"We have waited. As you have said, I am old.''

"We?" Vinn asked.

They saw a dimly lit room that extended away into what seemed to be infinity. Oblong objects with transparent domes lined each wall. They, too, extended forever, perspecting away until walls and domed oblongs merged together at the limit of vision. It was not possible to look into the clear-domed containers. There was movement and it was as if they flew down the center aisle of the room into the distances only to turn and soar through still another long room filled with the same oblongs from which glowed soft, yellow lights.

"Together we will decide if it is time to waken them."

The computer screen was blank. There were no induced images in Vinn's mind. He turned away from the console, his face white. "Waken them?" he whispered.

"Let them sleep," Sarah said, "for when they awaken the universe will tremble."

"Listen," Pete said, "don't fight it. We are they who have come."

"With all due respect," Vinn said, "cynical humor is just a bit out of place."

"Yes, sorry," Pete said. "Look, I'm going down there, whether any of you go with me or not. There's too much at stake. A new source of cheap power. And have you thought that what that thing can do—speaking directly into our minds—just might open up a totally new method of communications?"

"We have assumed that Mom and Pop Webster were lured down to the surface by the high metallic readings," Vinn said, "and that the others went down to reclaim the bodies of their dead. Are we to be lured down by the promise of great wealth and power through new technology?"

"Vinn, it's talking to us," Iain said. "It thinks we are the fulfillment of some kind of prophecy. Look, aside from a few little tricks of telepathy and this gravity thing, the weapons we've seen are pretty primitive. Fusion engines. Solid fuel missiles. A short-range laser.''

"But it flew the *Erin Kenner* into a sun," Vinn said.

"We can handle anything it has to dish out," Iain said. "Hell, it's nothing more than a super computer.''

"More than that," Vinn said. "It's a self-repairing, self-perpetuating artificial intelligence. The best estimates of the destruction of the Dead Worlds now range into the millions of years. We're dealing with something that's older than our civilization, older even than man on Earth.''

"I'll go with you, boss," Iain said.

"And I," said Kara.

"Vinn?" Pete asked. "I'd feel better if you were along. You're the computer man, after all.''

Vinn nodded. "I'll have to admit that I'm more than curious.''

"We'll take the two atmoflyers," Iain said.

The atmoflyers were two-place vehicles powered by small flux engines and armed with both sappers and laser cannon.

"At least one person stays on board," Iain said. He took Kara's hand. "I'm afraid it'll have to be you, love, because if something goes wrong down there, I want someone on the ship who knows all of her systems.''

"Yes," Sarah said. "I want to go. I want to see this thing. I want to understand why it killed all of my family.''

Neither Pete nor Sarah were proficient in the operation of scout-type atmoflyers. It was decided that Pete would ride with Iain, leaving Sarah with

Vinn. The two vehicles dropped away from the *Crimson Rose*, engaged flux engines to drive them into the thin atmosphere, dropped to hover over the circular opening. The cavernous room below was brightly lit. The metal walls and floor were devoid of markings or features. Iain's flyer settled to rest first. Vinn put his vehicle down nearby. He had the flyer's weapons ready. The iris of the hatch closed quickly over them.

"You will find the air to be to your needs," the Watcher said to them. "I will signal you when the pressure has been brought up to Earth normal. You may then remove your E.V.A. gear so that you can be comfortable."

"I think not," Vinn said.

"As you will."

Vinn didn't wait for the Watcher's signal that pressure had been raised in the chamber. He cracked the hatch of the flyer and let the vehicle's instruments test the air. It was pure, and rich in oxygen.

At the end of the chamber an irised opening appeared. "Come, please," the Watcher said.

Iain led the way, saffer rifle in hand. Pete and Vinn carried hand weapons. Sarah moved awkwardly in the heavy gear. They walked down a blank corridor. A door opened into a room that was furnished oddly but attractively. A woman in a silver gown that reached to her shapely ankles stood up to smile at them.

"Goddamn," Iain said in surprise.

The female voice was pleasant as it spoke English. "If I make you uncomfortable—"

"Not at all," Pete said. "You're very attractive."

"I am nothing more than an extension," she said.

"You are the Watcher?" Vinn asked.

"Yes. I felt that you would be more at ease if I spoke with you in this form."

"May I?" Vinn asked, stepping close. The woman held out her hand. It was smooth and cold. "In whose image are you formed?"

"In the image of they who have come."

"We're here," Pete said. "You said it was time to talk. We're ready."

* * *

The Watcher was, of course, able to function on many levels. Physical contact had been established with the orbiting ship. Lines of force now connected the Watcher with the *Crimson Rose*. As the extension smiled and talked with the four who were inside, it was a simple matter to send a significant fraction of the energy of the planet's field into the mind of the one who monitored the instruments on board the ship. The force detonated inside the skull of the female, shattering bone and turning her brain into a pale gray soup.

CHAPTER SEVENTEEN

The Watcher, in the form of a maturely attractive woman, waved one hand gracefully toward chairs arranged in a conversational circle. Vinn Stern nodded at Pete and Iain and set the example by accepting the Watcher's invitation.

Sarah de Conde sat on the edge of her chair, her hands in her lap. She stared at the Watcher with her eyes squinted belligerently.

The material that covered Vinn's chair made a dry, crackling noise as he lowered his weight. The furniture was functionally simple in design and made for the humanoid form. As Vinn leaned back and crossed one leg over the other, a faint whiff of age and dry rot emanated from the chair.

The walls showed a faint geometric pattern. Light came from a glowing square in the ceiling, which was an expanse of otherwise unbroken white. In the center of the circle of chairs was a low table on which sat a free-form sculpture. Pete de Conde picked up the piece, judging it to be carved from a stone very much like marble.

"I am sure you have questions," the Watcher said, through the extension. "If, however, you will allow me to speak, I think that most of them will be answered.''

"We are your guests," Pete said, inclining his head toward the extension.

"It is in the intent of creation that each living thing consummate the purpose for which it was intended." The extension leaned forward slightly and spoke in a low, intense voice.

"What gives you the right to speak for creation?" Sarah demanded.

The Watcher ignored the interruption. "Life is the apogee of the cycle of cosmic evolution and no one form of life is more favored than others. I'm sure that you think me wrong, for you consider yourselves to be the penultimate achievement of creation and evolution. I say penultimate rather than ultimate because you are not content with life as it was given to you. You cling to the belief, or the hope, that there is something after this life, that you are destined to evolve into an even higher form. Once you were so certain of this uncertainty that you manipulated your genes to take the form of that to which you aspire.''

"Are you speaking of the fossil remains of winged beings on Erin Kenner's world?" Vinn asked.

The extension nodded, causing her dark hair to sway forward onto her cheeks. "An excellent example of perverting the intent of creation. Of course, such blatant manipulation of form and intent had disastrous effects on the mental balance of the winged ones.''

"That's very interesting," Iain said, "but what does it have to do with us?"

"As far as we know," Vinn said, "our race evolved on one planet, Earth."

"Be patient, and you will understand," the Watcher said. "Your narrowness of vision is another of your weaknesses, but your most serious fault is the result of your having postulated for yourself an exalted existence after death. By relegating your life to secondary importance, you have given yourselves an avenue of evasion down which you can travel to rationalize away your failure to accept the responsibilities that are inherent to the living."

Vinn was being very human. Resentment toward the Watcher's condescending lecture made him bristle. "You know so much about us in such a short time?" he asked.

"I know enough," the Watcher said. "You told me that you are familiar with only a small portion of this galaxy, but you send your exploration ships into unknown areas searching for that rarest of treasures, a planet which can support life; and when you find such a planet what do you do? You immediately begin to alter the balance that nature has developed."

"Is this wisdom your own, or was it implanted by your creators?" Vinn asked. "Because if you're forming your opinion of our entire race from what you've learned from a few individuals, you have only a tiny piece of the picture. You speak of balance, but the balance changes. It is natural for a newly evolving species to compete with an established species and there can only be one winner. Of course, a growing population of humanity on a world alters that world. That in itself is the nature of things."

"The problem is that you actively and often maliciously attack the symmetry of creation," the Watcher said. The extension fixed her large blue eyes on Vinn. "In nature, development of a particular species can be looked upon as somewhat experimental. It's as if creation says—ah, let's see if this will work. Sometimes it works, sometimes it doesn't, but if a species vanishes it was not the experiment that failed, but the subject of that experiment. You overturn the entire scheme of things by, in effect, taking over the experiment yourself. You are not content to live in your environment, you change it to suit your desires at the moment. Let me give you an example. Through you I know the planet you call Terra II. It has taken centuries of effort to even partially repair the damage you did to it."

"That was thousands of years ago," Vinn said. "And speaking of altering the environment, what do you call what was done to this planet?"

"It is not necessary to justify the actions of the Creators," the Watcher said. "However, I will tell you that eradicating life from this planet was a part of the restoration of balance. Unlike what you did to your Earth, the actions taken by the Creators were essential. You know so little about your own mother planet, but you do know that you soiled it, used it up, and then charred it. You made it unfit for life except in its lowest forms."

"You know Earth?" Vinn asked.

"Only through your knowledge of it, but I can describe it to you. Once it thrived with living things. Creation has a talent for seeking out and filling with life all possible habitats. There were millions of species of vegetation. There was an extravagant diversity of animal life and bird life, not to mention insects and microbes and other microscopic forms. Then evolution produced you and you altered the experiment. You lifted yourselves beyond the purpose for which you were intended. For just such a situation have we been waiting.''

"You have been waiting to do what?" Iain asked.

"We will discuss that," the Watcher said.

"How long have you waited?" Vinn asked.

"No matter, you have come. Now we must decide."

"We can't decide anything with nothing more than hints about you and your purpose," Vinn said. "Before we attempt to make any heavy decisions, we have to have the answers to a few basic questions."

The extension nodded.

"First, tell me how you regard yourself."

"I am that which was created."

"By whom?"

"By the Creators."

"Do you consider yourself to be a living entity?"

"From your own mind I find the phrase: I think, therefore I am."

"That's an evasive answer," Vinn said.

"You would call me a machine."

"A thinking computer with the ability to reason and learn?"

"Yes."

"Therefore you were manufactured, put together, by someone like us, someone who breathed oxygen, someone who was flesh and blood."

"Yes."

"Who were your creators?"

"Yes, you would have to ask, wouldn't you? You have no way of knowing."

"No, we don't know," Vinn said.

"I was created by you."

Pete, who had been leaning forward eagerly, sat back with an audible sigh of exasperation.

"And the Sleepers," Vinn said. "Who are they?"

"They are what you would have been."

"Would have been if what?" Vinn asked in exasperation.

"Excuse me, Vinn," Pete said, "isn't this just so much mumbo jumbo? Let's ask this thing why it killed my wife's family."

"I will answer that question. Those who trespassed were silenced because, as I have pointed out to you, it is the intent of creation that each life-form be allowed to perform its purpose."

"I'm sorry," Vinn said, "that doesn't make sense. Those who came to your planet were, at least in their view, going about a purpose. It's the nature of mankind to seek knowledge."

"It has been your nature to disregard the intent of creation, to interrupt the natural process, to destroy, to alter. The Creators saw this and took steps to restore the balance."

Vinn wiped a film of nervous perspiration from

his forehead. It was easy to forget that the lovely woman who smiled at him so caringly was nothing more than metals and plastics. The way she— or it—was lecturing them told him that the Watcher considered itself to be superior, but there was a chilling irrationality in its reasoning.

A world had been, somehow, wiped clean of life and then turned into a frozen fortress to guard what seemed to be a force of cosmic enforcers of a doctrine that not only questioned but prohibited human achievement. There was no time to think through the hints and tidbits of information that the Watcher had thrown out, but it was evident that the Watcher and its creators believed that the development of life was common in the galaxy, and that the end result of creation, or the evolution of life-forms, was man, or something so like man that there was, in the Watcher's awareness, no difference.

Of course, they were curious, the four who sat on the age-dried coverings of the functionally designed chairs and listened to the words of the Watcher coming from the lips of an imitation of life in the form of a beautiful woman. But there was an underlying implication of deadly danger that made Vinn want to look over his shoulder. He had used the finely tuned sensors of the E.V.A. suit's gloves to touch the smooth, artificial skin of the female who sat demurely opposite them. There had been no life there. The skin was cold and unfeeling. She was nothing more than an extension of a machine, and he was beginning to think that that machine, the Watcher, was not rational or—equally as dangerous, that those who had made the machine and set it to make life and death decisions in the name of keeping nature's balance had been psychopathic to the point of believing that it was their duty to commit genocide in the name of a natural balance.

There was an air of tension in the stark room. Vinn felt as if he should be doing something, that time was running out.

"I'd like for you to explain that last statement," Vinn said. "Just how did those who made you restore the balance?"

"You have seen," the lovely woman said with a slight smile, and into Vinn's mind sprang the images of the dead worlds spinning their way through eternal emptiness.

On the hand holding his rifle, Iain's knuckles went white. "Vinn," he said, "I think it's time we started looking for an exit."

"Not yet," the Watcher said. "It has not been decided." The extension rose. "Now you will come with me."

"Not just yet," Vinn said. "Why did the Creators destroy those planets we call the Dead Worlds?"

"To restore the balance in that segment of the galaxy," the Watcher said.

"Men like us lived on those worlds?" Vinn asked.

"Yes."

"You have accused us of being insensitive, of doing damage to worlds, of depriving other species of the right to fulfill their purpose. How can you justify the slaughter of billions of people?"

"When you administer a drug to cure yourself

of an infectious illness you destroy billions of units of life to restore the equilibrium within your own personal system,'' the Watcher said.

"If you think that comparing mankind to a virus is original," Pete said angrily, "you're crazy."

"It was, I felt, an analogy you could understand."

"We may understand more than you give us credit for," Pete said.

"Vinn, let's go," Iain said nervously.

"Not just yet," Pete said.

"Come," said the extension, moving toward the door to the chamber.

Vinn followed the extension into a long corridor. He tensed, and his hand was on the butt of his weapon. Iain bumped into him, lifted his saffer rifle. Dozens of silent, still, metallic, anthropoid forms stood with their backs against the walls.

"They are not animated," the Watcher said.

The extension led the way to a low-slung, open-topped vehicle with multiple seats, took her place at the front and motioned for the others to join her. When everyone was seated the vehicle moved silently and swiftly, passed through a circular port that closed behind them. They were in one of the infinitely long, narrow rooms that had been shown to them. Soft light glowed through the transparent domes of the containers arrayed along the walls.

"The Sleepers," Vinn said.

The silent vehicle flashed past hundreds, thousands of the containers, but the seats were so low that Vinn could not see into the domes. The vehicle turned and sped past the arched openings to other container-filled rooms. A door opened. The vehicle stopped just inside. One wall of the large room was covered with screens, instruments, dials. At the base of the wall a console ran full length with what appeared to be work stations at intervals. Although there was no sound other than those made by themselves, there was a feeling in the air somewhat like standing next to the housing of a blink generator when it was fully charged. Placed in rows were mechanical and electronic constructions, most of them with a seat attached.

"The Creators were very much like us," Vinn said to the extension of the Watcher.

"Of course. It is the pattern of evolution."

"And you, the Watcher," Vinn said, waving his hand toward the far wall, "you are here."

"Because an accident might cause some damage," the extensions said, "you will relinquish your weapons."

"Not a chance," Iain said.

A door opened and one of the metallic, animated extensions entered the room. Iain tried to raise his rifle, but his arms were paralyzed. Pete was also helpless.

Vinn felt the intrusion of the Watcher into his mind. He fought against it, and with a great effort managed to put his hand on the butt of his hand saffer and lift it from its holster. That was the limit of his ability.

"The animated extension will take your weapons," the Watcher said.

"No," Sarah said. She moved quickly, jerked the saffer from Vinn's hand, pointed it at the advancing robot. The heat of the blast warmed her face as the extension halted, a huge hole blasted into its middle.

Sarah turned, trained the saffer on the female. "We will keep our weapons."

"If you had missed the animated extension, great damage would have been done," the female said.

Sarah aimed the weapon at the control wall. "Get out of our minds or I'll blast every instrument on that wall."

"All right," Pete said, lifting his rifle. Iain turned a full circle, rifle at the ready.

"Perhaps you are responsible enough to be allowed to keep your weapons," the Watcher said.

* * *

For the first time the Watcher was unable to form a conclusion. That the woman was able to resist control was not logical. Only the Creators were strong enough to resist once initial penetration had been accomplished. One thing was certain. It had been a mistake to take those who had come to the Center. The one called Vinn had, quite surprisingly, recognized the control panel for what it was, and even while the Watcher ran the question through its center again and again Vinn was examining the keyboards, guessing at the function of switches, and coming very close.

The Watcher had the ability to learn, but over the eons of time since the beginning some of the Watcher's perceptiveness had eroded. Perhaps that was why there was indecision, although the

Watcher could not know guilt nor the fear of failure. When there was a thing to be done, it was done. The Creators were, of course, infallible. What they had intended to be would be. Everything they had predicted had come to pass. They had known that the process of creation was a universal constant, that sooner or later others would be in their image and that, once again, the balance would be affected. The Creators had erred only in their estimation of the amount of time that would be required for the selfish ones to evolve again and in not foreseeing that, so quickly, at least some of those who would come would have reached the Creators' own state of development. If, indeed, that last were true, the Watcher's task was simple. The Sleepers would have to be awakened. But it was necessary to be absolutely sure before taking that irrevocable step.

* * *

It was obvious to all that the Watcher was speaking directly to Sarah. "You, too, have responsibilities."

"That is not to be defined by you," Sarah said heatedly.

"Ah, but you are wrong. Only I can do so."

Sarah felt dizzy, fought it off, knowing that the Watcher was trying, once more, to control her. She thought of home, and her children, and the images of their faces burned away the feeling of infringement. She waved the saffer warningly.

"So be it," the Watcher said. "It is time. You

have made the decision, Sarah. You and you alone.''

"I don't know what you are talking about," she said.

"They will be awakened," the Watcher said, "but first we must determine whether or not you are worthy of knowing them."

The extension moved to stand beside an installation consisting of a comfortable chair and a framework of metal from which hung an appliance very much like an old-fashioned hair dryer. "I think, Sarah, that you would be of the most interest. Will you sit down, please?"

"No," Sarah said.

"You refuse to cooperate?"

"We are not subjects for experimentation," Pete said.

"Then the decision as to your worth must be made without complete data. I will have to decide based on the information I have."

Pete raised his saffer, pointed it at the control wall. "I don't think you could stop me before I pulled the trigger," he said.

* * *

The Watcher was silent as oceans of data swarmed into the Center and was examined without conclusion. The extension stood as if frozen, eyes blank, lips parted in a smile. The trespassers would not cooperate, therefore they were not as evolutionarily advanced as it had first appeared. There were puzzling contradictions. Certain aspects of their technology were impressive. The female was able to resist penetration, and the man called Vinn could do the same to a lesser extent. That was the most enigmatic thing about them. Did their science and the female's mental abilities offer threat? Raw data continued to churn through the Center, being checked and rechecked. The conclusion was that it was impossible for the trespassers to be where they were, or to exist at all. The development of intelligent life was a process that required time, time measured in geological eras. But they were there, and for a moment or two it had appeared that it would be necessary to awaken the Sleepers, but there was another solution.

"I have decided," the Watcher said. "Not only you, but the worlds you have infested will be silenced."

* * *

Vinn felt cold enter his body through the E.V.A. suit. Suddenly his toes ached, and he shivered. He tried to cry out, but he could not make a sound. He knew that he was under attack, and that the threat to his life was coming from the Watcher. His mind shouted, "No, I will not allow this."

The terrible cold penetrated to his bones. Out of the corner of his eye he saw Pete and Iain topple to the floor. They fell stiffly, like cut trees. Sarah's scream was in his ears and there were huge, crashing noises and the smell of heated metal and things burning as Sarah's saffer flared. The female form of the extension was caught in the full force of the weapon. Her midsection disappeared. Her head and torso fell to the floor. The lower body stood, balancing on long, smooth legs from which the silver gown, also cut in two by Sarah's blast, slowly sank to the floor. The exposed groin was smooth, like that of a doll.

The control wall buckled. Smoke filled the room. Vinn was able to move his head. He saw Sarah's face through her visor. Her white teeth showed in a snarl.

Vinn fell to his knees beside Pete de Conde. The liquid in Pete's eyeballs had expanded while freezing. There were skin lesions where rapid expansion had ruptured cells.

"You don't understand," the Watcher said in a flat voice that reverberated in the room. "You must not resist. You will feel pain only for a moment."

Sarah moved to stand over Pete's body. She looked down into his ruined face and cried out in loss and anger.

"You should not have caused such terrible damage," the Watcher said. "Some of what you have done is irreparable."

"Sarah, we have to go," Vinn said.

"What about my husband?" There were no tears. Not yet. Her face showed nothing but fury as she stood over the bodies of Pete and Iain.

"We can't carry them," Vinn said. "We have to get out of here and do what we should have done in the first place, call in X&A."

"I can't leave him. I can't leave him."

"Sarah, X&A will recover the bodies," Vinn said, taking her arm. For a moment she resisted, then, weapon at the ready, she followed him.

The corridor outside the Center was blocked by

four of the mechanical extensions. Vinn fired without hesitation, swinging his weapon back and forth on full beam until the way was cleared. The vehicle that had brought them to the Center was gone. Vinn led the way down the corridor and into the first of the long domed container rooms. The glowing containers could contain nothing other than the Sleepers.

"Entry is forbidden," the Watcher said.

Vinn stepped to the side of one of the domes. "My God," he said. Beside him Sarah shivered.

Tubes of some imperishable material were attached to the thin, sere arms of a wasted, mummified humanoid form.

"I have decided," the voice of the Watcher said, echoing away into the distance. "They must awaken."

Vinn moved on to the next dome. There, too, death had visited in remote times. From one of the tubes that terminated under the parchmentlike skin of the mummy a drop of clear liquid oozed. There was a puff of steam as it was quickly evaporated.

Sarah jumped convulsively as a sound of whirring machinery came from within the container. A robot arm moved toward the mummy's neck. A long, gleaming needle was protruded. The whirring sound came from all of the domes, from the hundreds that were visible, dwindling in apparent size with distance.

"They awaken," the Watcher said. "I have miscalculated. You are a danger. Now your death will come, for these are the Sleepers, the terrible ones, the irresistible ones who once before restored the balance. They will destroy you as they destroyed those of you who came before you, and they will destroy you and the worlds you have fouled and all that you have created.''

Vinn ran from dome to dome, saw only desiccated death. Attempts by the robot arms inside the domes to find a vein in the shrunken necks were resulting in robotic confusion. Long, gleaming needles searched, touched the withered skin, withdrew.

''Let's go,'' Vinn said, taking Sarah's arm. They ran back to the corridor, then in the direction from which they had come originally. In an alcove sat a vehicle much like the one that had brought them to the Center. Vinn helped Sarah into it, jumped in himself. He had watched the extension's operation of the vehicle on the way out. He pushed buttons. The vehicle sped down the corridor. He tried to remember which gallery led to the chamber where the aircars waited, but all of the arches looked the same. He picked one and sent the vehicle speeding between the rows of domed containers. The whirling sound of the robotic machinery filled the long room.

''Whoa,'' he said, his heart leaping as he saw that the containers ahead were open. He pushed the button that stopped the vehicle. As far as his eye could see, the domes had been opened. Sarah's hand was shaking as she swept the empty aisle ahead with her saffer. Vinn leapt out of the vehicle and ran to look into one of the open containers. There was only the dry-rotted material of the pad on which a body had once lain. It was the same with the next few that he examined. In one there lay bones thinly covered with black, desiccated skin, but all of the others that he examined were empty.

He ran back to the vehicle. "If they were awakened, it was a long time ago," he said.

"No," said the Watcher's voice. "You're wrong."

* * *

But where were they, the Creators? The Watcher had taken the irrevocable step. The signal to activate the awakening procedure had gone out from back-up reason chambers. Monitors showed that the system was working, although the Watcher had most of its chambers engaged in assessing the damage done to the Center.

Where were the Creators? It had become obvious that the trespassers represented danger, that the balance was being tilted once again. Now the Creators would act. First the two remaining vermin would be exterminated, and then –

"It will do you no good to make ridiculous statements," the Watcher said.

"Your Sleepers are dead, Watcher," Vinn Stern said. "And these, several hundred of them, it appears, were awakened long ago."

"That is impossible. They are here," the Watcher said.

"Damn it, use your sensors," Vinn said. "Look, this dome has been open so long that the pad has atrophied. "Look." He pressed the bottom of the container. Where his gloved hand touched, the material turned to dust.

The Watcher saw through Vinn's eyes. "Hundreds of them?"

"At least. The opened lids extend ahead of us as far as I can see."

The vehicle was moving at speed again. A blank wall ended the gallery. Vinn turned the vehicle around and sent it flashing back toward the corridor. He regretted the wasted time.

"What's that sonofabitch up to?" he whispered to Sarah. In a loud voice he called out, "Watcher, they're all dead or gone."

The Watcher did not answer. The intruders were still alive. Something was wrong, for it was not logical that the Creators were awake and that those who had done such terrible damage to the Center were alive.

Vinn turned into another gallery. At the end of it, a distance of miles, a circular port opened. The two aircars sat in the center of the large, empty chamber. He helped Sarah out of the vehicle and led her at a clumsy run toward the aircars. He hit the switch that started the flux engine as he fell into the pilot's seat. Sarah was half-in, half-out when he tilted the aircar and triggered the laser cannon to boil away the metal hatch overhead. The air rushed out of the chamber as the aircar leapt for the sky.

CHAPTER EIGHTEEN

Although deeply wounded and blinded throughout large areas of the core installations, the Watcher was functional. Animated extensions were ripping away the damaged modules and replacing them. Top priority was assigned to repair of the sensors in the halls of the Sleepers. The Watcher could not know the emotion of dismay. There was only an acknowledgment of receipt of data when newly installed circuit boards reported the fact that certain sensors in the halls had been inoperative for an indeterminate but significant length of time.

Monitoring ability fully restored, the Watcher recorded the same reading from ninety-nine percent of all Sleeper units. They were dead. They had been dead for a period of time that could not be measured. Only a few hundred of the units did not contain the mummified, desiccated remains of the Creators, those who had been preserved to guard the balance. The hoods of those few hundred units stood open. Power to the nurturing containers had been turned off.

It was the Watcher's function to learn. As the ability to see was restored, there was another discovery. In the fleet storage area half a dozen starships were gone. Someone had tampered with the sensors that kept the Watcher apprised of their state of readiness. For eons the sensors had been reporting false data. It could only be concluded that the few hundred Creators who had been awakened long ago had departed the planet aboard the missing starships, after having rigged the sensors to send erroneous signals.

If the Watcher could have felt emotion, it might very well have known loneliness. They were dead, all the Creators, or they had left long, long ago. If the Watcher had possessed human qualities, it might even have felt a sense of futility, for it had been guarding nothing more than itself; but the Watcher was a machine, a thinking machine, true, but a machine. It operated with cold, irrefutable logic. It had been created to do a job. Whether or not the Creators were dead, or gone, had no relationship to the duty that had been assigned to their creation. In fact, it was logical to think that it was the intent of creation, the Creators having proven to be nothing more than fragile flesh and blood, that the eternal creation carry on their work. The balance was in danger at best, had already been impacted beyond redemption at worst. The Watcher had been created to guard the balance. Therefore, it was the Watcher who would restore order to the galaxy.

The number of worlds in the United Planets Sector was considered. As communications links were restored, assignments went out to fleet units. In subterranean chambers all over the planet start-up units drained power until the fusion engines of thousands of small drone ships were humming quietly. From the fusion engines, power was fed to the smaller units that generated the fields that would blend with the planet's far-diffused gravitational waves and make it possible for the ships to move instantly from one point to another on the continuum of the wave. The Watcher calculated routes for each of the ships and checked each of the small, gravity-lock missiles that were the vessels' only weapon.

The small missiles, shaped for driving through atmosphere, represented the highest technological achievement of the Creators. The weapon had been developed as a backup for the Creators' own abilities. It was relatively crude. It could not sterilize a world and leave it rolling in its orbit. It could only fragment and destroy, but the end result was the same.

Somehow a new strain of pre-Creators had spread with totally abnormal swiftness over a sizable segment of the galaxy, overwhelming the balance. The situation would be corrected.

Meanwhile, there remained only one small detail to be handled. Now that the two who had done so much damage were out of the underground complex, they could be handled easily. The power that could not be applied inside the installation, lest function be disrupted in all gravity-driven units, was now available for use again. Before silencing the last two of the trespassers, however, the Watcher would recheck through their minds and the memory of the computer aboard their ship the locations of all U.P. worlds.

* * *

Sarah de Conde seemed to exist on two levels. Inside, in quivering, agonized waves that threatened to break through and overwhelm her, was the knowledge that almost everyone she loved was dead. Her husband, her mother and her father, her two brothers and two sisters, all of them were dead at the hands of that thing back there below the ice. In that guise, as bereaved woman, she wanted only to be alone with her sorrow, to let the hot tears come; but she was another person, as well, and in that persona there was fury. She was furious that at some time in the distant past beings very much like herself—if the Watcher was to be credited—had decided that they and they alone had the answers, that in their superiority they had the right not only to exterminate billions of lives in the name of some bullshit theory about the quote "ecology" unquote, and, indirectly, although her father and mother and Joshua and the others were not, of course, known to them, to decide to kill no less than half a dozen members of the Webster family.

She spoke only in answer to direct questions from Vinn as the aircar soared upward and tucked itself into the lock of the *Crimson Rose*. Vinn, puzzled and alarmed by the lack of response to his calls from Kara Berol, hurried from the lock to the control room, his saffer in hand, to find Kara's body.

"I don't think you want to see this," he told Sarah as she entered the bridge.

'Oh, yes, I do," she said, kneeling beside Kara. This latest death merely fed her fury.

"But how could it reach her here?" Vinn asked.

"If it can do this at such a distance, why was it necessary to lure the others to the surface?"

"I will answer that question before you are silenced," the Watcher said through the ship's communicator. "It was necessary to establish a link between your ship and my instruments before the power could be used. That link was made when you touched down on the surface."

Vinn felt the beginning of panic. He had a semblance of resistance to the Watcher's penetration of his mind, but he had seen what had been done to Kara and he was frightened. He knew that he was very close to death.

"Watcher," he said, "it's over. Your Creators are dead."

"My duty continues," the Watcher said. "You will activate your computer."

"Do it," Sarah said, her eyes blazing.

Vinn pushed buttons. Sarah leaned past him and wrote on a notepad.

BUSTERS.

He nodded. The computer was ready. The Watcher was there, inside. Vinn's heart pounded as the spatial coordinates of all U.P. worlds flashed rapidly across the screen. He began to punch buttons himself, holding his breath. One by one the fail-safe barriers to arming the planet busters were negated. Sarah stood by his side, her teeth bared in tension.

"Now I have all the information I need," the Watcher said.

Three steps remained to arm the planet busters.

"Wait," Sarah said. "If you kill us, you will be killing your Creators."

"My Creators are dead."

"Not all of them died," Sarah said, her eyes watching Vinn's fingers as they flew over the keyboard. "Some of them were awakened early. Where did they go? You, yourself, said that our rise was too swift. That puzzled you. But if the Creators who were awakened early settled other planets, wouldn't that explain the fact that I can keep you out of my mind?"

There was a long period of silence as the Watcher deliberated that question. Sarah felt the dizziness indicating that the Watcher was trying to enter her mind. She rejected the effort, her anger giving her strength.

A shrill tone of warning came from the weapons system. A screen flashed. The planet busters were armed and ready. Vinn set about overcoming the firing fail-safes.

"We are your Creators," Sarah said, as she watched Vinn's fingers. "And as your Creators we order you to cease your vigil. Your duty has been done. The balance is not endangered."

"You gutted and ruined your original planet of settlement," the Watcher said.

"We have restored Terra II," Sarah said. "It is true that we used up her resources during the centuries that it took for us to rebuild a technology and to get back into space, but we have healed the scars we left."

"Millions of species perished."

"There was only vegetation on Terra II when our ancestors landed there," Sarah said.

"Only rank weeds grow on your Earth," the Watcher said.

"We saved those who remained, the New Ones, the mutated ones. They are an integrated part of our society, quite valuable, as a matter of fact. The wrongs that our ancestors did were in the far past," Sarah replied.

"A moment in time," the Watcher said.

Sarah felt belittled by being forced to plead for her life, but it was not her life alone. She was thinking of her children.

"You think that you will persuade me to let you live," the Watcher said. "That is a vain hope. You, Vinn, you prepare some weapon to be used against me. That too, is futile. You will be ready to fire your puny weapon with two more keystrokes, but before you push the last key you will be dead. Not that your weapon could do more than minor harm. What will you do, destroy another of the freezer units? Blast through the ice and earth in an effort to reach me?"

"Do it," Sarah said.

Vinn punched a key. Now there remained only one final keystroke, a very simple one. He held his finger poised over the key.

"I will show you weapons," the Watcher said, and on the largest screen there appeared an image of a good, blue world. A tiny streak of light slashed down from the darkness of space. For long moments nothing happened, then the planet's crust swelled outward and ruptured.

Both Vinn and Sarah had seen the old film of the destruction of Zede worlds in the last space war. This was the same. The planet fragmented. The molten core flowed and shattered.

"Thus will I restore the balance," the Watcher said.

"You don't have the means," Vinn said, his finger poised, shaking, over the firing key.

Now the screen showed row after row of small ships. Ports opened.

"I will allow you to see the launching of the fleet before I silence you," the Watcher said.

"Now," Sarah said.

Vinn's finger plunged downward, but before it could touch his entire body went limp as the Watcher detonated power inside his skull so forcefully that the milky soup that had been his brain cracked his skull and forced itself out through the cracks, through his ears, through his nose and mouth and eyes. He sank to the floor.

Sarah screamed.

"Can you resist that?" the Watcher asked. "Can you resist that as you reject my presence?"

"I don't know, you son-of-a-bitch," Sarah said, "but we're going to find out." She moved her finger toward the keyboard. The alarm that warned of the readiness of the planet busters was loud in her ears. The firing light blinked glaring red. She steeled herself for oblivion, felt the Watcher's presence. She stabbed down with her finger and the ship shuddered as the missiles carrying the busters sped away, accelerating under power. She felt pressure inside her head, staggered. The viewscreen showed the two weapons burning a bright downward arc through the thin atmosphere of the ice planet, and then there was nothing.

* * *

The Watcher saw the two missiles leaving the orbiting ship and accelerate. Counter missiles blasted, but the oncoming weapons were past them and thundering toward the surface ice before the planet's defenses could react.

No matter. The damage would be minimal, even if the invaders had armed their insignificant weapons with thermonuclear warheads. That, the Watcher reasoned, would be the limit of the technical ability of the trespassers.

But why wasn't the woman dead?

* * *

Sarah sat up. Her hand went to her forehead. Her head ached fiercely. She looked up at the screen. She had not been unconscious long, for the busters were still driving down through atmosphere. She knew that on-board instruments were taking the measure of the planet. She knew, also, that she was in grave danger because she was too near. She was the last one left. Someone should go back to tell the story to X&A's scientists, but it was not duty to mankind that motivated her to live. Everyone was dead. Poor Vinn was dead. Only her children were left. That thing down there had taken from her everything but her children, and she was not going to let it take them from her through her death.

She was not sure that she was doing it right as she punched in a short blink. Even though she was in danger of dying with the Watcher's planet, she wanted to see that thing down there die, or, more properly, be silenced. She pushed the button and the *Crimson Rose* disappeared even as the on-board computers caused the diving missiles to vanish as well. The *Rose* came back into normal space at a distance of two hundred thousand miles. It took Sarah a few seconds to activate the screens.

The ice planet swam serenely in the darkness of space, sun side reflecting light glaringly. Sarah adjusted the optics, compensating for the glare. She was able to see the first swelling of the icy crust. Not one but two weapons designed to destroy a world had blinked instantly to the planet's core.

The red of molten metal was seen briefly as the world shattered from the inside out. There was steam as ice melted and then the planet simply disintegrated into flying chunks of rock and cooling core material.

Sarah was breathing rapidly. Her head ached.

"You killed my mother, my father, my brothers and sisters," she whispered to the dying world. "You killed my husband and my friends."

She believed in a divinity, if not in the preachers who took it upon themselves to be spokesmen for God. She prayed, as she watched the particles of the deep freeze planet go their separate ways, that those who had made the Watcher were now burning in an old-fashioned Christian hell.

She buried Vinn and Kara in space, sending them off toward the sun with the words of the ancients. She spent a few hours making sure she understood the process of locking onto a distant blink beacon. The *Crimson Rose*'s generator was fully charged when she punched a button and, with a sigh of relief, found that the ship lay quite near the first of the *Rimfire* beacons.

She was going home. It would be up to X&A to worry about whether or not there were other Watchers. She had things to do. She found it difficult to believe that she'd left her children in the care of others for so long, even if they were with her closest friends. She knew, rationally, that she had been influenced by the Watcher's spatial extensions, but that was no excuse. Her first duty was to her children.

And then there was the election that would be coming up in less than four years. If she started her campaign very soon after getting back home, she'd be in fine shape to be elected. She had three young ones in T-Town schools. They deserved the best education available and she intended to see that they got it. After all, they would need all the knowledge they could absorb to insure that the human race would survive if the U.P. worlds ever encountered the Sleepers who had long ago awakened and vanished.

DAW

Epic Tales of Science Fiction

James B. Johnson

☐ **A WORLD LOST** UE2498—$4.50

Rusty was a spacer, one of the last of a dying breed. Now, returning home to find his entire solar system gone, Rusty had no choice but to turn to the hated government bureaucracy for help, only to find himself faced with a conspiracy of silence surrounding the disappearance of his world. Rusty's quest seemed totally hopeless until he stumbled upon the one secret which the government would do anything to preserve—the knowledge that humankind had at long last been contacted by an alien race. . . .

Zach Hughes

☐ **MOTHER LODE** UE2497—$4.99

Back from space, Erin found her father dead and herself heir to a mining tug called *Mother Lode* and a set of coordinates which might open the way to unbelievable wealth—or a doom beyond any human's imagining. For what awaited at her journey's end was a mystery far older than the human race. . . .

Betty Anne Crawford

☐ **THE BUSHIDO INCIDENT** UE2517—$4.99

In a future in which Japan economically dominates the Earth, the past and the present are constantly being "rewritten" by their paid Historians. But So Pak, son of Earth's finest Historian, seeks another path—the path of "freedom." Seeking to learn the truth about two lost mining expeditions, he launches a mission on the starship *Bushido*. But someone is determined that neither So Pak nor the *Bushido* will ever return to Earth.
